P9-CAM-414

"But terrorism and violence as a way of life?" the reporter pressed. "It seems a rather harsh way to extract a living from the universe."

"Terrorism and violence," Tambu mused. "Yes, I suppose you could call it that. Tell me, though, Mr. Erickson, do you apply the same phrasing to what the Defense Alliance does? Both my fleet and that of the Alliance earn their living the same way: selling protection to the planets. They include us as one of the threats they are protecting the planets against. Aside from that, we do not differ greatly . . ."

For the first time, the man known as the "Interstellar Genghis Khan" tells his story. Believe it or not, as you choose. A man in Tambu's position does not need friends, though he may take a theoretical interest in the world's assessment of his veracity . . .

TAMBU

ROBERT LYNN ASPRIN

ACE SCIENCE FICTION BOOKS
NEW YORK

TAMBU

An Ace Science Fiction Book / published by arrangement with
the author

PRINTING HISTORY
Ace trade paperback edition / November 1979
First mass market printing / August 1980
Second printing / August 1985

All rights reserved.
Copyright © 1979 by Robert Lynn Asprin
Cover art by Rowena Morrill
This book may not be reproduced in whole or in part,
by mimeograph or any other means, without permission.
For information address: The Berkley Publishing Group,
200 Madison Avenue, New York, New York 10016.

ISBN: 0-441-79744-X

Ace Science Fiction Books are published by
The Berkley Publishing Group,
200 Madison Avenue, New York, New York 10016.
PRINTED IN THE UNITED STATES OF AMERICA

TAMBU

INTERVIEW I

As the airlock door hissed shut behind him, the reporter took advantage of the moment of privacy to rub his palms on his trouser legs; he wished that he had a bit more faith in his Newsman's Immunity.

He had never really expected to be granted this interview. The request had been made as the prelude to a joke: a small bit of humor to casually drop into conversation with other reporters. He had anticipated making lofty reference to having been refused an interview by the dread Tambu himself. Then, as the skeptics voiced their doubts, he could silence them by producing the letter of refusal. But his plans had come to a jarring halt.

His request had been granted.

His editor had been no less surprised than he; his cynical indifference was swept aside by a wave of excitement . . . excitement mixed with suspicion. An interview with Tambu would be a feather in the cap of any journalist; a much-sought-after feather which had thus far eluded the grasp of many older, more experienced reporters. It seemed strange that this prize would

go to a junior reporter who in five years of working for
the news service had covered only minor stories.

One thing was sure: this interview would not be filler
material. It would be the turning point of his career,
eagerly read and studied throughout the settled universe, focusing an incredible amount of attention on his
work. If his treatment was equal to his subject, he would
be flooded with job offers. But if his work was judged
and found lacking . . .

Despite his daydreams and careful preparations, he
found that now that it was imminent, he approached the
meeting with increasing dread. There were a thousand
ways this "golden opportunity" could sour, resulting in
an abrupt end to his career . . . and perhaps his life with
it.

He had half-expected, half-hoped, that when he arrived at the rendezvous, he would be greeted by empty
space. But the ship had been there, dwarfing his own
craft with its immense size. The reporter remembered
being slightly disappointed at the outward appearance
of the vessel. He had expected a sleek jet-black monster
adorned with Tambu's well-known crest . . . the silver
death's head surmounted on a nebula. Instead, the ship
was little different from the hundreds of freighters
which traversed the starlanes, shuttling their cargos
from planet to planet. The only clues to this ship's
potential savagery were the numerous gun turrets
prominent on its outer hull. It seemed ready for combat,
its sails taken in as if in preparation for flight or fight
. . . though the idea of his tiny ship attacking this
dreadnought was ludicrous.

Now, here he was aboard Tambu's own flagship,
about to meet face to face with the most feared individual in the settled universe. He had only a moment to
reflect upon these thoughts before a soft chime sounded
and the inner door opened to receive him.

The first thing that struck him about the quarters was

the psychological warmth of the room. He instinctively wanted to examine the quarters more closely, and just as instinctively suppressed the desire. Instead, he contented himself with a brief look at the cabin and its contents.

The walls were of a texture unfamiliar to him, of a dark gold in dramatic contrast to the customary white. The trappings of the room made quiet contribution to the atmosphere. There were paintings on the walls, and books lined the shelves—honest-to-God books instead of the tape-scanner usually found in libraries and studies. Several easy chairs were scattered about the room, obviously at convenient points for reading or contemplation. Tucked away in one corner was a bed—double bed, the reporter noted with professional interest.

The only reminder that this was not simply a luxury cabin or a lounge was a huge communications console which dominated one full wall of the room. Even compared to the familiar network terminals at the newscenters, this console was impressive, with banks of keys and controls surrounding a modest viewscreen. After eyeing the console's array of flickering lights and gauges for a moment, he turned again to sweep the cabin with a wide gaze, seeking an overall impression.

The total effect of the room was quite different from what the reporter had expected. It had the lived-in, personal air of a home, rather than the cold efficiency of a command post. Anywhere else it would have been incredibly relaxing. Here it gave the room the feeling of a lair. The reporter glanced about him again. Where was Tambu?

"Please be seated, Mr. Erickson."

Startled by the voice, the reporter turned again to face the console. The viewscreen was still blank, but it was apparent that the unit was operational, and that Tambu was now watching him . . . watching and waiting.

Fighting off his apprehensions, the reporter seated himself at the console.

"I am addressing Tambu?" he asked with an ease he did not truly feel.

"That is correct, Mr. Erickson. I notice you've brought a Tri-D recorder with you. As I will not be meeting you face to face, it is unnecessary. The console at which you are seated is recording our conversation. You will be supplied with a copy. Visually, there will be nothing to record."

"I was promised a personal interview," Erickson half-explained, half-protested, then cursed himself mentally. If he didn't watch himself, he'd end up alienating Tambu before the interview even began.

"Personal in that you will be dealing with me directly rather than with one of my subordinates," Tambu clarified, apparently unoffended by the reporter's remark. "For security reasons, a face-to-face meeting is out of the question. I maintain several flagships identical to the one you are on now, and part of the problem confronting any Defense Alliance ship seeking to capture me is discovering which ship I'm on and when. My exact location is kept secret, even from my own fleet."

"Aren't these precautions a little extreme for meeting a lone reporter in a rented shuttlecraft?"

"Frankly, Mr. Erickson, reporters have been known to stray from their oaths of neutrality . . . particularly where my fleet and I are concerned. My defensive preparations for this meeting, therefore, go quite beyond what meets the eye. As an example, you might be wondering why you were granted this interview aboard one of my flagships when the smallest ship at my command has a viewscreen you could have listened at just as easily."

"It did cross my mind," the reporter admitted uneasily. "I assumed you were trying to impress me."

"There was that," Tambu laughed, "but there was

also another, much more important reason: all my flag-ships, including the one you're on now, are rigged to self-destruct either from the captain's cabin, or by a remote signal from me. The explosives on board are sufficient to cause severe damage to any ships in firing range at the time of detonation. If your request for an interview had been a ploy to lure me or one of my ships to a predetermined point for an ambush, the appearance of a dreadnought-class flagship would have been a nasty surprise for the hunters. If the waiting ships were of sufficient size or numbers to trap and capture a dreadnought, the captain was under orders to trigger the self-destruct mechanism. It would have been a costly but necessary example for anyone who might entertain similar thoughts of entrapment."

"I thought the crew seemed awfully glad to see me," Erickson muttered, licking his lips nervously. "So I'm sitting here on a bomb that might go off at any time. That's certainly incentive for me to keep this interview short."

"Please, Mr. Erickson, there is nothing to worry about. I mentioned the self-destruct mechanism as an example of our defensive arrangements, not as a threat to you. Take as much time as is necessary."

"If you say so," the reporter murmured doubtfully. The conversation was taking a dubious tack, and he was eager to change the subject.

"You're upset," Tambu observed. "If you'd care for a drink, there is a bottle of Scotch on the table by the bathroom sink, along with glasses and ice. 'Inverness' I believe it's called. Feel free to help yourself."

"Thank you, no. I don't drink while I'm working."

"Very well. However, I've taken the liberty of order-ing the ship's crew to load a case of that particular liquor onto your ship. Please accept it as a personal gift from me."

"You seem to know quite a bit about me," the reporter

observed. "Right down to the brand of liquor I would drink, if I could afford it."

"I probably know more about you than you do, and definitely more than you'd like me to know. I've reviewed your family history, health records, psychological records, as well as copies of everything you've ever written including that rather dubious series of articles you wrote in school under an assumed name. You were checked very closely before permission for this interview was granted. I don't talk with just anyone who drops me a note. In my line of work, my whole future and that of my forces hinges on my ability to gather and analyze data. If I didn't think you were safe, you wouldn't be here."

"Yet you refuse to meet me face-to-face and dispatched a ship rigged to blow in event of betrayal?" Erickson smiled. "Your actions aren't as confident as your words."

There was a moment of silence before the reply came.

"I've made mistakes before," Tambu said at last. "Often enough that I long since abandoned any ideas of infallibility. In lieu of that, I guard against all possibilities to the best of my abilities. Now may we start the interview? Even though I have tried to set aside time for this meeting, there are many demands on my time and I can't be sure how long we'll have before other priorities pull me away."

"Certainly," Erickson agreed readily, glad to resume the familiar role of an interviewer. "I guess the first question would be to ask why someone of your intelligence and abilities turned to the ways of war and world conquering as a way of life rather than seeking a place in the established order."

"Purely a matter of convenience. If you think for a moment, I'm sure you could think of several men both as intelligent and as ruthless as I in your so-called established order. As you pointed out, they have successfully risen to positions of power, wealth, and influence. I am not that much different than they; only I chose to move into a field where there was little or no competition. Why fight my way up a chain of command when by taking one step sideways I could form my own chain of command with myself at the top, running things the way I felt they should be run from the start instead of adapting someone else's system until I was high enough to make my presence felt."

"But to terrorism and violence as a way of life?" the reporter pressed. "It seems a rather harsh way to extract a living from the universe."

"Terrorism and violence," Tambu mused. "Yes, I suppose you could call it that. Tell me though, Mr. Erickson, do you apply the same phrasing to what the Defense Alliance does? Both my fleet and that of the Alliance earn their living the same way—selling protection to the planets. They include us as one of the threats they are protecting the planets against. Aside from that, we do not differ greatly, except in words; a 'police action' versus a 'reign of terror.' Perhaps I over simplify the situation, but I don't feel the differential is justified."

"Then you see nothing wrong in what you're doing?" the reporter asked.

"Please, Mr. Erickson, none of your journalistic tricks of putting words in my mouth. I did not say I don't see anything wrong in what I do; simply that I don't see that much difference between my own forces tactics and those of the Defense Alliance."

"Are you then asserting that in the current conflict that it is you who are the hero and the Defense Alliance the villains?" Erickson prodded.

"Mr. Erickson I have asked you once, I will now warn you," Tambu's tone was soft, but deadly. "Do not attempt to twist my words into what I have not said. If I make a statement or express an opinion you take exception to, you are certainly welcome to comment to that effect, either in this meeting or in your article. However, do not attempt to condemn me for opinions which are not my own. I have shown my respect for you and your intelligence by granting this interview. Kindly return the compliment by remembering that in this interview you are not dealing with a dull-witted planetary sub-official and conduct yourself accordingly.

"Yes, sir. I'll remember that," the reporter promised, properly mollified. He would have to mask his questions more carefully.

"See that you do. Still, you did raise a curious point. The rather romantic concept of heroes and villains, good guys and bad guys. It would be amusing if I did not think that you actually believe that rot. That's the main reason I granted this interview. It stands out all over your writing, and I wanted to meet someone who really believes in heroes. In exchange, I offered you a chance to meet a villain."

"Well, actually . . ." Erickson began, but Tambu cut him off.

"There are no heroes, Mr. Erickson. There are no villains." Tambu's voice was suddenly cold. "There are only humans. Men and women who alternately succeed and fail. If they are on your side and succeed, they are heroes. If they're on the other side, they're villains. It's as simple as that. Concepts such as good and evil exist only as rationalizations, an artificial logic to mask the true reasons for our feelings. There is no evil. No one wakes up in the morning and says, 'I think I'll go out and do something terrible.' Their actions are logical and beneficial to them. It's only after the fact when things go awry that they are credited with being evil."

"Frankly, sir, I find that a little hard to accept," Erickson frowned. This time his challenge was planned, carefully timed to keep his subject talking.

"Of course. That's why you're here, so I could take this opportunity to show you a viewpoint other than that to which you are accustomed. As a journalist, you are no doubt aware that in the course of my career I have been compared with Genghis Khan, Caesar, Napoleon, and Hitler. I believe that if you could have interviewed any one of those men, he would have told you the same thing I am today, that there is no difference between the two sides of a battle except 'them and us'. There may be racial, religious, cultural, or military differences, but the only determination of who is the hero and who is the villain is which side he's on. That—and who wins."

"Then what you are claiming is that this moral equivalence of opponents also applies to today's situation?"

"Especially today," Tambu said. "Now that mankind has moved away from the bloodbath concept of war, it is easier than ever to observe. Despite the blood-curdling renditions of space warfare which adorn the newstapes and literature, actual combat is a rarity. It's far too costly in men and equipment, and there is no need for it. Each fleet has approximately four hundred ships of varying sizes, and there are over two thousand inhabited planets. Even at the rate of one ship per planet, there is always going to be over eighty percent of the planets unoccupied at any given time. For a ship of either force to move on a new planet means temporarily abandoning another. As such, there is little or no combat between the fleets. The objective is to either move into unoccupied systems and divert their tribute into our coffers, or move into an occupied system with sufficient force to where the opposing ships will abandon the system rather than enter into a lopsided battle. It's a massive game of move and countermove, with little if any difference between the gamesmen."

"A stalemate," Erickson suggested. "Yet there was a

time when the Defense Alliance was substantially weaker than your fleet. I find it interesting that you were powerless to stop its growth.

"Just because we refrained from openly opposing the Alliance when it was forming doesn't necessarily mean we were powerless to do so. You might say that was my error. I seriously underestimated their potential at first and actually ordered my fleet to avoid contact with them. Remember, we were well established at the time, and did not consider them a serious threat."

"I remember," the reporter nodded. He didn't, but he had done his homework in the news-service's backfiles. "Actually, I had hoped to get some information from you about those early days, before the Defense Alliance formed."

"That would take quite a bit of time, Mr. Erickson. I don't think you're aware of what you're asking. Most people never heard of me until we first started offering our services to the planets. In actuality, the fleet had been operating as a unit long before then. For me, the early days go back much farther than the point when we first appeared in the public eye."

"But that's specifically what I'm after. I want to be able to trace your career from its early days to the present, showing how you've developed over the years."

"Very well," Tambu sighed. "We'll cover as much as time allows. This will probably get quite involved, but I'm willing to talk if you're willing to listen."

"Then how would you say your career began?"

There was a moment's pause.

"There is a strong temptation to say I started out as a child."

". . . born into a poor, but honest family?" Erickson completed the old joke, smiling in spite of himself.

"Not really. Actually, my parents were fairly well off. Various people have speculated that I had a bitter childhood, ruthlessly fighting for existence in the streets of some backwater planet. The truth is my father was . . . successful, quite successful at what he did. I would even go so far as to say that I had more love and affection in my early childhood than did the average person."

"Then . . . what happened? I mean, why did you . . . choose the path you have?"

"Why did I turn renegade?" Tambu asked, echoing Erickson's thoughts. "First, allow me to clarify my home situation. While, as I said, I was not lacking for affection, there were certain expectations placed upon me. I was to exceed my father's achievements—a task which, I assure you, was not easy. It seemed that everything I set my hand to, my father had been there first and done it better."

"So your father's pressure eventually drove you out," Erickson prompted as Tambu paused.

"Not directly . . . nor intentionally," Tambu corrected. "Much of it was self-imposed pressures or expectations. When I flunked out of college—undergraduate studies, at that—I decided to strike out on my own rather than return home. This was done partly because I was ashamed to face my parents, and partly to make a name for myself as myself, not as my father's son."

"I must admit you've succeeded there," the reporter smiled, shaking his head ruefully. "So you ran away to space. Then what?"

"I worked tramp freighters for several years. I had a friend . . . a close friend. He was several years older than I, and gentle as a kitten for all his strength. We worked several ships together, and probably would still be doing just that except for the mutiny."

"The mutiny?" Erickson's attention focused on the story possibilities.

"Not in the sense you're imagining. There was no organized revolt, no dark conspiracy. It just happened. Unfortunately, I can't give you the details without seriously breaching security . . . both my own and the forces'."

"Couldn't you omit specific details and change the names?" the reporter pleaded.

"Possibly . . . Actually, the important event was not the mutiny, but the decision we reached shortly thereafter."

CHAPTER ONE

The plump, red-faced man filled the small captain's cabin with his indignant anger, barely leaving room for his adversary seated behind the desk. This was not unusual. He was Dobbs of Dobbs Electronics, a man who fought his way to the top and who wasn't about to let anyone forget it—not his relatives, not his employees, and definitely not the captain of some second-rate tramp freighter.

His noisy indignation was his trademark, as was his presence for this transaction. Other business owners would sometimes relax and enjoy their success, delegating menial tasks to their subordinates, but Dobbs was cut from different cloth. He had been there for the unloading, riding the cargo shuttle from the ship to the spaceport planetside and back again. He had personally delivered the payment for the shipment. Therefore it was only natural that he would feel obligated to personally handle this last detail.

None of the proceedings had met with his approval, but this last oversight was a particular annoyance. He was in the wrong and he knew it, but that knowledge only increased his bitterness. More than anything, Dobbs hated to be wrong. Never one to hide his feelings, particularly his anger, Dobbs let his displeasure show. It showed in his stiff bearing and tight lips, in his ruddy complexion, and in the abrupt way he slammed the attaché case down on the desk.

"There it is." he announced flatly. "The balance of payment. I believe you said fifteen thousand was the difference between the original purchase price and the price you're asking now?"

"That's not entirely correct," the man seated behind the desk said. "It constitutes the difference in currency exchange between the time of purchase and the time of delivery."

"Semantics," the visitor countered. "It's still costing my company fifteen thousand more than we planned."

"As you will." The man at the desk sighed. "Would you care to have a seat while I count it?"

"I'd rather stand."

The seated man had been reaching for the attaché case, but at his visitor's rebuke he hesitated, then sat back in his chair frowning slightly.

"Mr. Dobbs . . . it is Dobbs isn't it? Of Dobbs Electronics?"

The visitor nodded stiffly, annoyed there had been any doubt as to his identity. He had been dealing with this man off and on for three days now.

"You seem both upset and determined to express your annoyance by being rude. I find both positions difficult to understand."

Dobbs started to protest, but the man at the desk continued.

"First of all, when you ordered your materials Cash On Delivery, you accepted the risk of currency-exchange fluctuations. That is standard in any contract of that kind, but it's still good business. If you paid in advance and our ship was attacked and taken by pirates, you'd be out the full cost of the shipment. As it is, you have to pay only for goods delivered, even though occasionally you have to pay a premium."

"Occasionally!" Dobbs snorted. "It seems like every time . . ."

"And even if I felt the system was unfair, which I don't," the man at the desk continued, "this ship is only the means of delivery. We don't make the rules. We only shuttle materials from point A to point B and collect the money, as instructed. In theory, we shouldn't have allowed your men to unload your cargo until we had collected our payment in full."

The man was leaning forward now, his eyes burning with a sudden intensity.

"In short, Mister Dobbs, I feel we've treated you fairly decently through this entire affair. If you have a complaint, I suggest you write a letter. In the meantime, isn't it about time you came down off your high horse and started acting like a human being?"

Dobbs started to retort angrily, then caught himself, reconsidered, and relaxed, exhaling a long breath. Like most bullies, he would give ground when confronted by a will of equal or greater strength.

"I guess I have been making a bit of a jackass out of myself, haven't I?" he admitted ruefully.

"You have." The seated man opened the attaché case and began counting.

Dobbs responded by sinking into the offered chair and leaning forward, his elbows resting lightly in his knees. He had discovered in the past that people were more receptive when approached at eye level.

"I guess I forgot that the captain of a freighter is a businessman same as me." he confided. "You know, as much as we've seen each other these past couple days, I've never gotten around to asking your name. It's Blütman, isn't it? Ulnar Blütman?"

"No, it's Eisner, Dwight Eisner. I'm the First Officer. Captain Blütman doesn't like to handle the business end of things, so I take care of it for him."

"Isn't that a little strange?" Dobbs frowned. Usually . . ."

"Mr. Dobbs," Eisner sighed, "if you had treated Ulnar Blütman the way you treated me, I guarantee he would have broken your nose and dumped your goods out the nearest airlock. He is, at best, an unpleasant man."

"I see," Dobbs commented, taken slightly aback. "Say, are you taking cargo on before you ship out? Maybe I can put together a shipment for you. You know, to make up for the way I've acted."

"That won't be necessary. We already have a sizable load to pick up at our next stop."

He set the case aside abruptly.

"The count tallies. Just a moment and I'll transfer it into our safe and you can have your case back."

"Keep it." Dobbs waved. "Consider it a present. How much have you taken in this run, anyway?"

"Nearly a quarter of a million. A little less than average, but it's not bad."

"Quarter of a million?" In cash?" Dobbs was visibly impressed. "That's a lot of money!"

"I just wish it was mine." Eisner laughed. "Unfortunately, there are a lot of people waiting at the other end of the run to get their share. Our piece is ridiculously small considering the risks we take, but if we up our prices too much, the companies will buy their own ships and we'll be out of business."

"I suppose. Well, I've got to get going now. Watch out for pirates, and if you're ever back this way, look me up. I'll buy you a drink."

"I'll remember that." Eisner smiled, rising to shake the man's hand. "But don't even mention pirates. It's bad luck."

Dobbs laughed and departed, heading for the

shuttlecraft standing by to take him back to the planet's surface.

Eisner sank back into his chair. For long moments he stared thoughtfully at the wall, then he turned his attention to the attaché case on the desk, running his hands softly over the leather finish.

His reverie was interrupted by a lanky youth who burst through the door like an exploding bomb.

"How did it go?" he demanded excitedly. "Is everything all right?"

Eisner smiled tolerantly. Nikki always seemed to be going in eight directions at once, even under normal circumstances.

"It went fine, Nikki," he said reassuringly. "The nice man gave me an attaché case."

"He what?" the boy blinked.

". . . and the extra fifteen thousand." Eisner concluded, opening the case dramatically.

"You did it!" Nikki exclaimed. "God, you've got guts, Dwight. I never would have had the nerve to go for the extra. I was afraid he'd get suspicious."

"The man was trying to pull a fast one. He would have been more suspicious if we hadn't called him on it."

"I know, but—"

"Look, Nikki, it's just like I told you. If we just conduct ourselves as if the captain were still alive, no one will suspect a thing. This way, we've got the ship and a quarter of a million."

"But didn't he say anything?"

"As a matter of fact, he did." Eisner smiled. "He warned us to watch out for pirates."

"He did?"

Simultaneously, the two burst into laughter, whatever tension they had pent up finding release in the absurdity of the situation.

"Did I miss something?"

The interruption came from the middle-aged black

woman who had started to enter the cabin, only to stop
short at the laughter within.

"No, not really, Roz." Eisner assured her. "Did Dobbs
get off okay?"

"No trouble at all." Rosalyn sank into a chair. "He
seemed a lot politer on the way out than on the way in."

"We had a talk. I explained a few facts of life to him,
and he pulled in his horns a bit."

"That's nice," Roz grimaced. "Since you're in an explaining mood, maybe you wouldn't mind explaining a
few things to me—like what do we do next?"

"We already know that," Nikki protested. "Now that
we're pirates, we do whatever pirates do."

"Technically, we're mutineers," Eisner corrected.
"We aren't pirates until we actually attack another ship.
But Roz is right; we still have several options open to us
at this point."

"We've been through those already," Nikki grumbled.

"If you don't mind, Nikki," Roz interrupted, "I'd like
to go over them again. I'm not too wild about the choice
we've made so far."

Eisner began hastily, before a fight could start. "First
of all, we could continue business as normal. We could
return to our home port, report that the captain died of
natural causes in space, and run the freight business
ourselves. Of course, that would mean we'd have to give
the money we've collected to the proper people."

Nikki snorted derisively, but Roz silenced him with a
glare.

"Second," Eisner continued, "we could sell the ship,
divide the money among us, and either go our separate
ways or set up another business. The main problem with
that being that you need ownership papers to sell a ship,
and as soon as we touched down planetside, someone's
bound to get very curious about where we got our
money."

He paused, but the other two remained silent.

"Finally, we can play the cards fate seems to have dealt us. We can turn pirate and become one more ship gone bad, preying on the helpless and defenseless."

"You don't have to be so graphic on that last point," Rosalyn mumbled, half to herself.

"Of course I have to, Roz." Eisner insisted. "That's what anyone else would say about us. That's what we'll say about ourselves sooner or later. We'd better learn to live with it now while we still have other options. Later it will be too late to change our minds."

"You missed an option, my friend."

They all turned to face the massive figure framed in the doorway.

"You could all turn me in to the nearest authorities and pocket a hefty reward. They still pay pretty good for murderers."

"Abuzar, that isn't even an option," Roz scolded. "We've told you a hundred times, Blütman was an animal. If you hadn't lost your temper and killed him, one of us would have. We aren't going to turn you in for that."

"But I was the one who killed him," the big man insisted. "And now, because of me, the rest of you are going to become pirates. You can't make me believe that's what you really want to do, Roz."

"I can live with it." Rosalyn winced, turning away. "It won't be the first time I've earned a living doing something I didn't like."

"Not so fast!"

Eisner had been leaning back, his brows knitted.

"There's another option here, one we haven't considered before." His voice was tense with excitement. "It hadn't even occurred to me until Abuzar mentioned rewards."

"What is it?" Roz asked.

"None of us are too wild about becoming pirates.

Well, what if instead of becoming pirates, we hunt pirates? Besides what we get for salvage rights, there are bound to be businessmen who'll pay us if we can make a dent in the number of shipments and ships lost to pirates."

"Now you're talking!" Nikki exclaimed with the same enthusiasm with which he had accepted the idea of becoming a pirate.

"Pirates shoot back," Abuzar pointed out bluntly.

"But they're used to fighting freighters with little or no armament," Eisner countered. "If we're armed better than they are, with better sensors than normal so that we can see them before they know we're in the area, they're in trouble."

"Maybe." Abuzar conceded reluctantly. "But equipment like that could cost a small fortune."

"We've got a small fortune," Eisner shot back. "The first thing we'll have to do is find out what armaments and sensor equipment are available, and how much they cost."

"That's assuming we agree to take that option," Roz interrupted. "I seem to recall a few other choices."

There was an uncomfortable moment of silence. Then Dwight sighed.

"You're right, Roz. I guess the time has come when we have to make our final decision about the future. Anything after this is a commitment, and we shouldn't move unless everyone's in agreement. Speaking for myself, I'm willing to try being either a pirate or a pirate hunter, with preference toward the latter."

"I'm with you, Dwight." Nikki chimed in.

"I've got no choice." Abuzar shrugged. "Eventually someone will learn what I've done, and I'll be a hunted man. It's easier to run in space than on a planet."

"Well, Roz?" Eisner asked. "How about you? Are you with us, or do you want to shuttle down to planetside? We'll buy out your share of the ship if you want."

Roz chewed her lip thoughtfully for a few moments before she replied.

"Tell you what," she said at last. "You can count me in with two conditions."

"What conditions?" Eisner prompted.

"First, that we unanimously agree here and now that Dwight runs the show. That he becomes our captain officially."

"Why?" Abuzar asked suspiciously.

"Come on, Abuzar. You know as well as I do that there has to be one man at the top. Eventually we're going to be in situations where one person has to give the orders and make the decisions. I figure we should decide who that's going to be now, instead of arguing it out in the middle of a crisis. Dwight's been running things since Blütman died and doing a pretty good job of it. Nikki's too reckless, and even you don't trust your temper. I couldn't do it, and wouldn't want to if I could. To my thinking, that makes Dwight number one. If we can't agree on something as basic as that, we should call it quits right now."

"I don't think I'm all that reckless," Nikki grumbled. "But I've got no objections to Dwight running things."

"Abuzar?"

"If we need a captain, I guess Dwight's the logical choice."

"Okay, that's that." Roz nodded. "How about you, Dwight?"

"I guess I never thought about it. I'm like Abuzar. I didn't really think a chain of command was necessary for four people."

"But will you serve as captain?" Roz pressed.

"Before I agree, what was the other condition to your staying with us, Rosalyn?"

"Oh, that." Roz grimaced. "It's nothing really. Your agreeing to be captain was the big one. My second point was that I think we should all take new names."

"Oh, come on, Roz!" Abuzar exploded.

"Hold on a minute, Abuzar," Eisner said. "Why do you think that's necessary, Roz?"

"I don't know about you other space bums, but I've still got family out there. I'm not too wild about dragging their name into the crazy things I'm going to be doing, and I sure don't want some pirate tracking them down to get back at me. Besides, up until now we've all got pretty clean records. On the off chance that someday we want to quit what we're doing and go back to leading normal lives, it wouldn't hurt to have a 'clean' name to go back to. Whether the rest of you want to go along with this or not, I'm going to use a different name for my new career. From now on, I want the rest of you to get used to calling me 'Whitey.' "

"Whitey?" Eisner raised his eyebrows.

"That's right." She grinned. "All my life I've wanted someone to call me that. I guess this is as good a time as any to get it going."

"Whitey." Eisner repeated, shaking his head. "All right, what do you two think about the whole idea?"

"Puck." Nikki said thoughtfully.

"What was that again?" Eisner frowned.

"I said 'Puck,' " Nikki repeated. "That's what my dad always called me. It's the name of some cutsey-poo character in an old play. I always hated that name, but I like the idea of a feared pirate hunter called 'Puck.' "

"It fits you," Roz teased.

"It's no worse than 'Whitey,' " Nikki said.

"How about you, Abuzar?" Eisner asked.

"The only man who ever beat me in a fight was a retard they called 'Egor.' He couldn't count on his fingers, but I've never seen anyone fight like that. Yes, you can call me 'Egor.' I'd like that."

"How about you, Dwight?" Roz asked. "Are you going to get in on this?"

"Um . . . Dwight," Nikki said. "If you do, could you pick a name that sounds fearsome and ominous? I mean, you are going to be our captain, and it would help if you had a name that scared people when they heard it."

". . . and 'Dwight' just doesn't do it." Roz agreed. "What do you say, Dwight?"

"Actually, I'm not very good at names."

"How about 'The Skull'?" Nikki suggested hopefully.

"Be serious," Roz chided.

"I *am* serious," Nikki insisted. "His name should—"

"I think I've got one." Eisner smiled.

He had been doodling on one of the ship's receipt books, and held it up for the others to see. He had circled the logos: Ulnar Blütman's Moving and Transport.

"In honor of our departed captain who so generously left us his ship, I'll use the first letters of the old letterhead for my name."

"Ub-mat!" Nikki read. "I don't know, Dwight. It doesn't—"

"Reverse them. Reverse them, and what you have is 'Tambu' !"

"Tambu," Whitey echoed thoughtfully. "I like it. It's got a nice ring to it. Has it got any special meaning, or is it just a word?"

"There's no special symbolism." Eisner laughed. "It's just a name. Now that that's settled, I'm ready to give my first order as your new captain."

"Don't tell me, let me guess," Whitey quipped. "You want us to knock off the chatter and get to work. See how fast power corrupts?"

"Actually, I was thinking more in terms of breaking out a bottle of the good wine and toasting our new names and careers."

"And friendship!" Abuzar declared, clapping a massive hand on Eisner's shoulder. "You see, Roz? It'll take more than a new name or a new job to change this one. He'll always love his friends and his wine more than he loves work!"

They all laughed, though some laughed louder than others.

INTERVIEW II

"Ulnar Blütman's Moving and Transport?" Erickson asked, as Tambu lapsed into silence.

"Don't get your hopes up, Mr. Erickson." That was not a slip of the tongue betraying my original ship. It was a fabrication, as were the original names of the crewmembers, including my own. There is no—was no Ulnar Blütman. However, I assure you the actual origin of my name was equally inane."

"Well, what's in a name, anyway?" the reporter shrugged, hiding his disappointment.

"I assume you're being flippant, but there is an answer to that question. What's in a name is what one puts in a name. Tambu could have been a brand name for a new soap, but my actions and the legends which grew from them have made the name Tambu a household word of a completely different nature."

"You sound quite proud of yourself," Erickson commented dryly, unable to hide his distaste.

"That's another 'are you still beating your wife' sort of question," Tambu admonished. "But I'll try to answer it anyway. Yes, I am proud of myself. To get where I am today, I have overcome many obstacles and difficulties which would have stopped or crushed a lesser man. That is not boasting, merely stating a fact. I should add, however, that just because I am proud of where I am does not necessarily mean I am proud of everything I did to get here."

"Then you're ashamed of the things you've done?"

"Not ashamed, Mr. Erickson. Just not proud. There are certain events and decisions I regret in hindsight. Perhaps it is a rationalization, but I've never felt this type of regret was a trait unique to me. Surely there are things in your own past you wish you could do over?"

"There are," Erickson admitted.

"Then allow me to give you a bit of advice. Or rather, share a philosophy which has helped me when I find myself preoccupied with past mistakes. When I review a decision which turned out bad, I remember it was just that . . . BAD. "B" . . . "A" . . . "D". Best Available Data. I made the best decision I could, based on the data available, within the time perimeters allowed for the decision. Even though the results may not have gone as I predicted, or as I would have liked, I console myself with the memory of that moment of decision. Given the same situation, the same information, and the same amount of time to reach a decision, I would probably choose the same course of action again."

"That makes sense." The reporter nodded thoughtfully. "Thank you."

"Actually, it's an old accounting expression. But I find it applies readily to other fields as well."

"Getting back to an earlier statement," Erickson pressed, suddenly aware of the interview. "You mentioned having to overcome many difficulties in your career. While it is obvious they would be there, I can only imagine what they must have been. What were some of the specific difficulties you encountered?"

"They are literally too many to count, Mr. Erickson." Tambu sighed wearily. "At times it seems all I've encountered were difficulties. Sometimes I wonder whether I would have started this project originally if I could have looked into the future and seen the difficulties involved . . . if I had known then what I know now."

"Once you made that decision, how soon did you begin encountering difficulties?"

"Almost immediately. Things one takes for granted suddenly become obstacles when confronted by them directly. For example, there was the basic task of outfitting our ship for combat . . ."

CHAPTER TWO

"I don't like it, Dwight," Whitey cast a dark glance around the gloomy bar.

"It's Tambu. Remember?" He took a leisurely sip from the glass in front of him.

"I don't care if you call yourself the Queen of May," Whitey snapped. "I still don't like it."

The bar was a typical dive, indistinguishable from hundreds of its fellows which cluttered the streets around any spaceport. Its clientele was composed mainly of crewmen on leave and ground crews, with a few drab locals holding court at the grimy tables along the walls. A tired-looking whore was perched at the bar conversing with the bartender, her drooping breasts threatening to slip free of her low neckline when she laughed.

"I admit it's not what you'd call a class place," Tambu conceded. "But we're not here to deal with genteel folk."

"That's not what I meant," Whitey scowled. "I've been in worse places."

"Are you still worried about Puck? I don't like it either. Leaving a one-man watch on board ship is asking for trouble, but there wasn't any other way. All three of us had to be here for this deal: you for the technical expertise, me for the negotiating, and Egor for protection. It's dangerous, but it's the only way we could handle it."

"That isn't it, either."

"What then?"

"It's this whole business. When I agreed to go along with this pirate-hunter bit, I didn't figure it would mean skulking around like a common criminal."

"It's only a temporary situation," Tambu assured her. "Just until we get the ship outfitted. Until then we don't have much choice."

"Sure we do. We could buy our weaponry through normal channels, like other ships do."

"No we can't, Whitey. The kind of weapons we want can't be picked up through normal channels."

"But other ships—" Whitey began.

"Other ships buy antiquated weapons which haven't helped them at all in stopping a pirate attack." Tambu broke in pointedly. "We aren't cruising around hoping the pirates won't spot us, we're going to actively hunt them. For that, we'll need weapons as good or better than the ones the pirates use."

"I suppose you're right."

"I know I'm right. We've tried a dozen weapons dealers and gotten the same answer everywhere. 'Weapons of that nature are not available.' Then they try to sell us some popgun or other with toothy reassurances that it will be enough to protect us in most situations. Twice we've been told about the black market in arms here on Trepec, so here we are. If we can't find what we're looking for here, we'll just have to look somewhere else. We can't risk going into battle with inferior weapons."

"We could opt against going into battle."

"Not a chance," Tambu insisted. "The first time we try to move in on a pirate, they're going to fight—particularly if they think we're overmatched in the weapons department. I wish it wasn't the case, but that's the hard facts of the matter."

"What I meant was that we could decide to give up the whole idea of pirate hunting."

Tambu leaned back in his chair and studied her carefully.

"What's bothering you, Whitey? We've gone over this a hundred times. The four of us. You were in favor of it then, and now suddenly you're against everything . . . the weapons, the fighting, pirate hunting . . . everything. What happened? Have you changed your mind?"

"I don't know," Whitey admitted. "I was never that wild about the idea, but the three of you kind of swept me along—especially you, Mr. Tambu. You can be awfully persuasive. Now that we're actually moving on the plan . . . I don't know. I guess I'm just scared."

"You can still deal yourself out if you want to," Tambu offered gently.

"I'm not *that* scared." Whitey broke into a smile. "Who knows what kind of trouble you three would get into if I wasn't there to watch over you. No, I may grumble a lot, but I'm still in."

"You're sure I'm not 'persuading' you again?"

"I'm sure, but don't laugh about your power to convince people. I was serious about that. You have a way about you . . . I don't know what it is, that wins folks over to your way of thinking. If you weren't so honest, you'd make an incredible con-man."

Tambu protested, "I hate to argue with you, Whitey, but you're wrong. Maybe you're susceptible to my logic, but not everyone is. I remember a couple of girls—twins, in fact—that Egor and I made a play for on Isle, who weren't persuaded at all. Neither were their parents—or the police, for that matter. We were lucky our captain interceded for us, and he stepped in only because he didn't want to lose two crewmen—not because I convinced him to."

"Speaking of Egor, where is he?" Whitey interrupted, peering at the door. "Shouldn't he be back by now?"

"Don't worry about Egor. He can take care of himself. He's just not particularly good at keeping timetables. Except for that, he's dependable to a flaw."

"If you say so. There! You did it again!"

"Did *what* again?"

"Convinced me not to worry with just a few words. That's what I'm talking about. You could calm a cat in the middle of a dog show."

"Not any more than anyone else could. Sometimes I can, sometimes I can't. It's no big thing."

"You don't believe that any more than I do." Whitey snorted. "If you didn't think you had an edge on most people, why did you come along specifically to handle the negotiations on this deal?"

"Because I'm a little better with numbers than most. Except for that . . ."

"And you talk a lot better than most. You know when to push and when to back off. That counts for a lot."

"I suppose you're right," Tambu admitted. "But why make such an issue out of it? You have a feel for the mechanics of a ship that makes me feel like a kid. Each of us has something we can do better than someone else. So what?"

"The difference is I work with machines and you work with people," Whitey said. "I know what I'm doing and what to expect in the way of results. I don't think you do."

"Probably not," Tambu admitted. "But I still don't see why you should get upset about it."

"Because it's dangerous! You think you're only doing

what people want you to do, and never stop to think you're actually calling the shots. Just because we agree with you when you ask the final question doesn't mean we agreed with you when you started—"

Suddenly Tambu laid a hand on her arm, stopping her oration.

"Heads up! We're about to have company."

Three figures were approaching their table in a beeline course that left no doubt as to their intended destination. The girl was in her late twenties, sporting close-cropped blond hair, a halter top, shorts and sandals. The dusky-complexioned boy was in his early teens, and wore a sleeveless shirt open to the waist. Loose-fitting trousers and soft ankle-high boots completed his outfit. While there was nothing uniform about their garb, there was something in their gaze which set them apart from the other denizens of the bar and bound them together into a unit.

The man in the lead was of an entirely different cut. In his middle fifties, his hair was close-cropped which, coupled with his expression, gave him the appearance of a Caucasian Buddha. Mechanic's coveralls gave his short, stocky figure the appearance of butterball fat, but there was a feline lightness to his walk.

All three wore guns on their hips.

"Mind if we join you?" the leader asked, smiling as he reached for one of the vacant chairs at the table.

"As a matter of fact, we do." Tambu smiled back, hooking the chair with his foot and drawing it out of reach. "We're waiting for someone."

For a moment, the man's eyes narrowed, but the smile never left his face.

"No matter," he shrugged. "What we have to say won't take long."

"Good," Whitey commented dryly.

This time it was the man's companions who reacted, shooting dark looks at Whitey as their muscles tensed.

The leader, however, took the jibe in stride.

"A bit of a spitfire, isn't she?" he laughed, jerking his head at her.

"You said you had some business with us?" Tambu prompted, an edge in his voice.

The man nodded, showing even more teeth. "We've heard that you've been asking around after weapons of an exceptionally powerful nature."

"Where did you hear that?" Whitey asked sharply.

"Does it matter, as long as the information is accurate?"

"What makes you think it's accurate?" Tambu countered.

"The fact that she didn't deny it." The man smiled.

"Assuming for the moment you're correct, what business is it of yours?" Tambu asked. "Are you an arms dealer?"

The man threw back his head and laughed. "Me? Blackjack? An arms peddler? Not hardly." His laughter broke off and his eyes became wary. "And now that you've gotten that information out of me, maybe you wouldn't mind answering a direct question."

"Such as?" Tambu asked.

"Such as, are you a pirate?" Blackjack replied, his eyes darting weasel-like back and forth between the seated pair.

"No, we're not. If we were, we probably wouldn't admit it openly."

"Why not? I do. Blackjack's the name, piracy's the game. Been making a good living at it for over five years now. Now that I know you're not in the business yourself, I have a proposition for you."

"And what would that be?" Whitey asked, her curiosity getting the better of her.

"It's a straightforward deal. You tip us as to where you're going with your next shipment, we meet you, put a few picturesque but easily repaired holes in your hull, relieve you of your cargo, and we split the profits down the middle."

"You lost me with your logic somewhere," Tambu said. "Would you mind backing up and starting over?"

Blackjack rolled his eyes in exasperation. "Look, if you're not in the business, then you're looking for big guns to protect your cargo. If you're willing to pay that much for weapons, it stands to reason what you're protecting has to be pretty valuable. Right?"

"Keep going," Tambu replied noncommittally.

"The odds of your bringing a valuable shipment through are low, at best. You can't keep something that big a secret, and every space wolf around will be waiting for you. If you put up a fight, like it looks like you're planning to do, you'll probably not only lose your cargo, but your ship as well and maybe your lives."

"And so you're going to be generous and offer us a better deal," Tambu said wryly.

"Why not? If you do it my way, neither of us lose any men, and we both come out of it richer. Everybody's happy—except the insurance company that has to cover the loss. But they've got plenty of money."

He beamed at them, obviously delighted with his own cleverness. Tambu matched him smile for smile.

"No deal," he said flatly.

Blackjack's face fell.

"Why not?" he asked in a hurt tone.

"Just because we aren't pirates doesn't mean we're stupid. What if we give you our flight plan and run out the welcome mat when you show up. What's to keep you from shooting our ship and us full of holes and keeping the whole pie instead of just half?"

Blackjack was no longer smiling.

"I'll assume you aren't willing to take my word for it . . ."

"Good thinking," Whitey said.

". . . and instead I'll point out that it's in my own best

interest to keep this relationship going as a long-term business deal. Four or five halves add up to more than two halves, if you get my meaning.''

"Don't you think the insurance company would get suspicious after a while? Not to mention our customers?" Tambu asked.

"We could stagger it a bit," Blackjack explained, eager again. "Let a few shipments through and only hit the really big ones. By the time anyone figured out anything funny was going on, you'd have made enough to retire.''

"It's still no deal, Blackjack. I appreciate the offer, but I still think we're better off trusting in the guns we have pointed out than in the one pointed at us."

"You know what this means, don't you?" Blackjack rumbled, his expression darkening. "If we find you out there, it will be no quarter.''

"On either side," Tambu nodded. "Be sure your crew knows that before you come bareling in on us.''

"It's your funeral." Blackjack turned to leave.

"Just a second, Blackjack," Tambu called. "I have one last question before you and your playmates disappear.''

"What's that?" Blackjack scowled.

"What would you have done if we said we were pirates?''

"Then I would have told you to stay away from my territory. I don't take kindly to folks trying to horn in on my range.''

"And where is your range?" Tambu asked innocently.

"You'll find out when you cross it. Until then, just keep looking over your shoulder.''

"No harm in asking," Tambu shrugged.

The blond girl was whispering something in Blackjack's ear. He listened intently, a smile spreading slowly across his face.

"That's a good question. Those weapons you're after cost a lot of money. Do you have it with you, or is it on your ship?"

A sudden tension filled the air as the two forces surveyed each other.

"I don't think I'll answer that," Tambu said.

"Why not? It'll save us the trouble of finding out the hard way."

"Because the person we were waiting for just showed up," Tambu smiled, meeting the pirate's eyes squarely.

"Really?" Blackjack jeered.

"Really!" Egor answered, looming behind the trio, gun in hand. "These three giving you trouble, captain?"

"Trouble?" Tambu smiled at the frozen trio. "There's no trouble here. As a matter of fact, these three were about to put their weapons here, on the table, and go have themselves a drink. Isn't that right, Blackjack?"

The pirate nodded, tight-lipped, and eased his gun from its holster, placing it carefully on the table. One by one, the other two followed suit.

Tambu pointed. "I think that table there will do, where we can see you—and do keep your hands above the table, hmmm?"

"I'll remember this," Blackjack growled, leading the group away to the table.

"What was that all about?" Egor asked.

"That was some of the oppostion," Whitey explained. "All of a sudden, I'm a lot more eager to see them through a set of gunsights."

"Speaking of that, did you find your contact?" Tambu interrupted.

"Sure did," Egor nodded. "He's waiting outside. I left him there when I saw the crowd at your table. He seems to be the nervous sort."

"Well, bring him in," Tambu ordered. "The quicker we get this done with, the better I'll like it."

"Do you think it'll be okay?" Egor asked, jerking his

head toward the seated trio glaring at them from across the room.

"I think so," Tambu said judiciously as he hefted one of the guns from the table and glanced pointedly at Blackjack. "Go get him."

The man Egor escorted back to the table was a bespectacled, balding wisp of a man who clutched his attaché case to his chest like a drowning man clinging to a life jacket. His eyes kept darting nervously to the guns on the table as the introductions were made.

"There—there won't be any trouble, will there?"

"Relax, Mr. Hendricks," Tambu assured him. "Everything is under control."

"For an arms dealer, you seem awfully nervous around guns," Whitey observed.

"Just because I sell weapons doesn't mean I like to be around when they're used," Hendricks snapped defensively. "If I had my way, I'd deal only through the mail."

"Quite understandable," Tambu nodded. "Now then, Mr. Hendricks, if you could begin going over the weapons specs with Whitey here, I'd like to have a word with Egor."

The man nodded and began unsnapping his case as Tambu drew Egor aside.

"Egor, I have a couple of errands for you."

"I thought I would be here for the bargaining," the big man frowned.

"So did I, my friend, but this is more important. Get down to the spaceport and find out all you can about Blackjack's ship."

"Who?" Egor blinked.

"Mr. Personality at the table over there. Get a description of his ship if you can, and relay the information to Puck. Tell him to stand by the guns and open fire if that ship comes anywhere near ours."

"But our guns aren't good enough to fight off an armed ship!"

"I know, but until we close this deal, they're all we've got. If my guess is right, Blackjack's crew won't be too eager to get into a fight if he isn't there calling the signals."

"You'll keep him here? Then why do I have to—"

"He might be wired for sound," Tambu broke in. "If anyone on his ship picked up our conversation, they might be getting very curious about us."

"They might be going after Puck right now!" Egor exclaimed.

"Right! So hurry. There's no time to argue."

"Okay, but watch that table. I don't trust them."

"Me neither, my friend," Tambu admitted, but the big man was already on his way.

With a sigh, Tambu joined Whitey and Hendricks, pulling his chair around to where he could watch Blackjack's table without moving his head.

"Sorry to be so long," he apologized. "How are we doing here?"

"Hendricks has what we want." Whitey leaned back from the table. "Compatible with our ship's systems. If they were any bigger, we wouldn't have the power to fire them."

"That big?" Tambu said. "Where'd they come from?"

Whitey answered, "As near as I can figure, they were salvaged from some of the old Planet Tamer ships. Nobody else used guns that big."

"Professional ethics require that I never reveal my sources—or customers," Hendricks commented.

"How would these weapons stack up against their armaments?" Tambu asked, indicating the trio glowering at them.

"Blackjack?" Hendricks asked, peering over his glasses. "You'll have half again the range of anything on his ship."

"Fine," Tambu nodded. "And now the big question. How much?"

Hendricks produced a small notepad and scribbled briefly on it.

"I dislike haggling," he announced, pushing the pad across the table. "This is a firm price, including installation."

Tambu glanced at the figure on the pad and smiled.

"Let's be realistic, Mr. Hendricks. We want to buy the guns *without* a ship attached—used guns, at that."

"In mint condition," Hendricks countered. "Warehousing them has cost me dear."

"Which is all the more reason for you to be eager to sell them," Tambu pointed out. "And there can't be much demand for them if you've had to carry them in inventory this long."

Hendricks began to protest, but Tambu held up a restraining hand.

"Fortunately, I also dislike haggling. Here is my top offer, and we'll install them ourselves."

He crossed out Hendrick's figure and scribbled a number of his own on the pad.

"Ridiculous!" Hendricks scoffed, looking at the pad. "Just because I deal with pirates doesn't mean I'll stand still for being robbed myself. I'll let the guns rust away before . . ."

Tambu smiled to himself as he listened to the man's orations. Despite the volume and bitterness of his objections, Hendricks had not moved from his seat after examining their offer.

They would reach an agreement soon.

INTERVIEW III

"It sounds like you were getting it from all sides in the beginning," Erickson commented. Sympathy was always a good ploy to loosen a subject's defenses.

"Yes, we were quite alone then. Still, that is not particularly surprising. We were setting a new pattern, and change is always resisted. The people we dealt with were constantly assuming that we fit in the order they already knew. Our only consolation was that if they had realized then what we were about, they probably would have treated us much more harshly."

"How do you figure that?" the reporter urged.

"Well, I've always felt Blackjack could have given us more trouble, but he didn't. Pirates are not the devil-may-care adventurers people think they are. Even though they risk their lives in combat, they're usually very careful about the reward they are gambling their lives against. Before we armed our ship, we would have been easy prey for a ship such as Blackjack's, but there was no reason for him to fight us then."

"How about vengeance? You embarrassed him in

front of his crew there in the bar. Wouldn't he want to get even for that?"

"Vengeance is an expensive habit, Mr. Erickson. It's a luxury few businessmen can afford, and for all his flaws, Blackjack was a businessman. No, he believed us to be cargo haulers and decided it would be better to wait until sometime when he caught us with a full cargo hold. If he realized our actual plan of becoming pirate hunters, he probably would have attacked us at the earliest opportunity."

"You make it sound as if a confrontation between your ships was inevitable. I should think it would be a long shot at best."

"Not really," Tambu corrected. "While space itself is vast, there are a limited number of settled planets, and even fewer which have substantial space traffic in and out. Most ship-to-ship encounters occur in orbit over a planet rather than in space. If both our ship and Blackjack's were prowling the heavily trafficked lanes, it would only be a matter of time before we collided— especially if we were looking for each other."

"I see," the reporter nodded thoughtfully. "Getting back for a moment to your early difficulties, what would you say was the greatest obstacle you had to overcome?"

"Ignorance."

"Ignorance?" Erickson echoed, caught off guard by the abruptness and brevity of the answer. "Could you elaborate on that a bit?"

"Certainly. Our biggest problem was our own ignorance . . . naïveté, if you will. We were out to beat the pirates at their own game, but we had no real idea of what that game was. Blackjack was the first pirate we had met face to face, and we wouldn't have known it if he hadn't told us."

"And this ignorance hampered your early efforts?"

"It did more than hamper them, it crippled them. I've already given you an idea of how long it took us simply to find our suppliers. If any of us had crewed on a pirate ship, we would have had the information and known exactly where to go."

"But once your ship was outfitted, things started to go easier, right?"

"Quite the contrary. It wasn't until our ship was fully outfitted and we went hunting for our first opponent that we began to realize how little we knew about pirates. In many ways, that's when our real problems first began. . . ."

CHAPTER THREE

"How much longer until they can see us?"

As Puck's voice came over the intercom, Tambu punched the 'talk' button on his command console, not taking his eye from the two ships on the viewscreen.

"Stow the chatter, Puck." he ordered. "Just keep watching that upper turret.

As might well be expected, they were all nervous. The next few minutes could well be the culmination of nearly a year's preparations.

Refitting the ship had taken much longer than any of them had anticipated, not to mention costing considerably over the original estimates. The results were heartening, however. The ship, now named the *Scorpion*, had a sting to be reckoned with in the form of four long-range slicers. Hendricks had assured them that they were now armed better than any ship currently registered. The only discomforting thought was that not all pirate ships were registered.

Even more important than the weapons, and twice as costly, were the custom scanners which allowed them to appraise a situation from a position well outside the range of another ship's detection equipment.

That plus several months of practice made the Scorpion and her crew formidable opponents. When they were all in agreement that they were ready to do combat, a new problem arose. How do you find the pirates?

Their only solution had led them here, to the Weisner System, which reported the highest frequency of pirate attacks. Prepared for a waiting game, they had struck paydirt almost immediately. In orbit over Magnus, the largest inhabited planet in the system, their detectors found two ships lying side by side. One was disabled and showed signs of recent damage, while the other seemed to be unscratched, and had two turret guns prominently mounted on her exterior.

It could be a pirate in the process of looting a victim. Then again, it could simply be a commercial ship answering a distress call. The problem was one captains had been wrestling with for over a decade. How do you tell a pirate from any other ship until he fires on you?

A hurried conference among the Scorpion's crew yielded the current course of action. They would ease close enough to the two ships that their guns would be in firing range, but the smaller guns of the functional ship would be unable to reach them to return fire . . . hopefully. From that position, they would hail the ship, offering assistance, and try to determine the situation confronting them.

Of course, there were several precautions they took to insure their safety in the maneuver. First, they kept their solar sails furled, relying on their storage batteries for power. Although this meant less power for their weapons or for emergency flight, Tambu reasoned that the fighting, if there was any, would be over quickly one way or another.

They angled their approach so that they were not aligned with the guns of their potential opponent, thus guaranteeing themselves first-shot capability before any fire could be brought to bear on them. Finally, Egor and Puck were manning batteries of two guns each, keeping them closely trained on the turret guns of the ship they were approaching while Whitey handled the actual maneuvering of the *Scorpion*. Tambu stood by ready to handle the talking once they opened communications.

They had taken every precaution possible, short of simply bypassing the entire situation. Both of the ships they were approaching had their sails out, obviously not combat ready in their vulnerability. Still the crew of the *Scorpion* were wet-palmed nervous—individually and as a group.

Another few minutes . . .

"Whitey?" Tambu asked abruptly.

"Yes, captain?"

"Am I set with a hailing frequency?"

It was a needless question, one that he had asked before. Tambu was no more immune to the strain of nerves than any of the others in his crew.

"Sure are, captain. They should be able to hear you now if you want to start."

They were within the range of the *Scorpion's* armaments now. Tambu knew that if he waited much longer, they would be vulnerable to return fire from the other ship. Licking his dry lips, he reached for the hailing microphone.

"Captain!"

At least two voices called to him from the ship's intercom, their exact identity lost in the garble of their overlap.

"I see it!" he barked. "Open fire!"

One of the turret guns on the functional ship they were approaching had begun to move, swiveling toward them in smooth silence.

Even as Tambu gave the order, the guns of the *Scor-*

pion opened up, the orange beams of slicers darting out like striking snakes toward their would-be assailant.

Though the crew of the *Scorpion* had practiced often and long with their slicers in mock attacks on small asteroids and occasionally on the face of an uninhabited planet, they had never seen the actual effect of their weapons on another ship. Now they had a front-row seat.

There was no explosion, no shower of sparks or flame. The portion of the rival ship which came into contact with the orange beams simply melted away like thin plastic before a soldering iron. One of the beams hit a sail, severing the tip. The remaining portion of the sail crumpled slowly as the severed tip began to drift away into open space. Both turret guns simply vanished, erased completely by direct hits from the slicers.

"Cease fire!" Tambu shouted, finding his voice at last.

The beams halted at the sound of his command, and silence reigned as they surveyed their handiwork.

The stricken ship's hull was already healing itself. The outer hulls on all ships were triple thickness with auto guidance to slide new plates into place in event of damage severe enough to cause interior pressure loss. Soon the exterior of the ship would be repaired. They could only guess at the interior damage of their attack.

Tambu's eyes wandered to the third ship, floating silently next to their recent opponent. Having now seen how fast a ship could heal itself after an attack, he could appreciate anew the extent of the attack which had wrecked such havoc as to leave a ship gaping open like that.

"We got him!" Puck's awe-filled voice came over the intercom.

"Keep your guns on him!" Tambu snapped. "We don't know if he has any more surprises up his sleeve."

"Captain?" Whitey joined the conversation. "Aren't you going to try hailing them now?"

There was something in her voice that caught Tambu's attention. In contrast to Puck's enthusiasm, Whitey seemed almost pensive.

"Is something bothering you, Whitey?" he asked.

"Well . . . it occurs to me that except for some shooting, nothing has changed." she replied hesitantly. "We still don't know whether or not they're pirates."

There was a moment of stunned silence. Then the crew erupted in protest.

"Cm'n, Whitey!" Egor groaned. "He was getting ready to shoot at us."

"That's right," Puck added. "He wouldn't have done that if—"

"Sure he would," Whitey interrupted. "Any of us would. If an unidentified ship came easing up to us with its sails in and its guns out, what would we do? We'd crank our guns around and cover the bastard until he said who he was and what he wanted. That ship couldn't have known whether or not we were pirates just like we didn't know if he was a pirate—and we still don't."

"What were we supposed to do?" Egor snarled. "Wait until he opened fire and cut us in half?"

"Whitey's right," Tambu said softly.

"But—captain—" Egor protested.

"She's right." There was a bitter firmness to Tambu's voice now. "We don't know. We've got to find out—if it's not too late. Whitey, are we still set for hailing?"

"Affirmative, captain."

Tambu slowly picked up the hailing microphone, hesitated, then depressed the transmission button.

"This is Tambu, captain of the Scorpion. Identify yourselves and state your condition."

There was no response.

"This is the Scorpion," he repeated. "We want identification of either or both of the two ships in our vicinity. Do you require assistance?"

It seemed strange, offering assistance to a ship they had been firing at a few minutes before. Still there was no response, nor was there any sign of movement from either of the other two ships floating on the viewscreen.

Setting the hailing microphone aside, Tambu flipped several switches on his command console, then settled himself in the swivel chair, one hand resting on a small keyboard.

"Egor!" he called into the intercom.

"Yes, captain?"

"I'm taking over your battery. Take a shuttle over and investigate that ship—the one we fired on. Check for survivors, and look for any records or logs to tell us what kind of ship she is. And Egor . . . ?"

"Yes, captain?"

"Go armed. Take along a hand communicator and stay in touch."

Then there was nothing to do but wait. Tambu keyed his mind to detect movement from either of the other two ships and blotted out everything else. Even when the shuttlecraft finally appeared on the screen heading out on its mission he did not comment or react. Instead, he thought.

Their procedure had been in error; yet there was no other course they could have followed. They had blundered forward, forcing a confrontation whether the opposing ship was a pirate or a legitimate commercial vessel. Even catching a pirate in the act, they were left unsure as to its identity or motives. Moving in blindly as they had done was wrong, yet they could not afford to let a pirate take the initiative. Just as in this encounter, if fighting was involved, whoever shot first and straightest survived. The other . . .

How could they identify a pirate? How did pirates operate? He'd have to think like a pirate. A pirate's main weapon would be his anonymity, not his guns. By approaching another ship under the guise of a distress call—perhaps a request for medical assistance or repairs—a pirate could strike the first and final blow before their victim was aware of its danger.

That only emphasized their problem. Scorpion couldn't wait to be fired on to identify her enemies. How to pierce the cloak of secrecy? How to anticipate . . .

Perhaps that was the answer. How did pirates know where to hunt? Surely pirates couldn't rely on circumstance to find ships to prey on. They needed some method to find target ships—specifically target ships with large, expensive cargos. If the Scorpion could find out how the pirates set their traps, if they could anticipate where the pirates would be and be there waiting for them, then they might have a chance.

But how were they to find out how the pirates operated?

"You're awfully quiet, captain." Whitey's voice interrupted his thoughts.

"Just thinking, Whitey," he replied absently.

"You aren't blaming yourself for what happened, are you? Heck, we all had a part in it. If we made a mistake, we're all at fault."

"That's right." Puck's voice chimed in. "You didn't even do any shooting. Egor and I were the ones who jumped the gun."

"At my command," Tambu said pointedly. "Just as we moved in on the ships at my command."

"But like Whitey said," Puck insisted, "we all had a part in it—the planning and the execution!"

"Ships aren't run by committee," Tambu reminded him. "That's why you made me captain. Besides getting the lion's share of the glory and profits when we do well and having last say on policy, being captain means that I hold the bag if things go wrong. It goes with the job. Isn't that right, Whitey? You were the one smart enough to dodge the captain's post. Wasn't avoiding responsibility one of your main reasons? Then don't lecture me about how I shouldn't feel responsible."

"I've got an answer to that," Whitey answered. "It's called the Nuremburg trials. The weight of responsibility falls on everyone in the chain of command, not just the one who gives the orders. If we were wrong, if we just shot up a commercial ship instead of a pirate, then we're pirates—all of us. If they catch us, they'll hang all of us, not just you, captain."

"Touché!" Tambu laughed. "But I wish you didn't have to be quite so morbid with your example."

"Not to change the subject, captain, but can we afford to get a few more viewscreens installed?" Whitey asked. Then we can keep one thing on the main screen and still have a couple of little ones for talking to each other. I don't know about you, but I like to see people when I'm talking to them. Otherwise I can't always tell if they're serious or joking."

"That will depend on what those two ships have on board," Tambu answered. "Whether we're pirate or pirate hunter, I figure we have salvage rights on both vessels."

"There should be a bundle after we sell the ships," Puck declared.

"We'll see," Tambu said.

"What do you mean, 'We'll see'?" Whitey asked, her voice suddenly sharp. "We are going to sell the ships, aren't we?"

"Egor to Tambu. Do you read me?"

Egor's voice blared suddenly over the console speaker, cutting off their discussion.

"This is Tambu. Go ahead."

"We're in the clear, captain. This is a pirate ship, all right."

Relief washed over Tambu like a cool wave, freeing his mind of its slowly building tensions.

"The ship's name is the *Mongoose*," Egor continued.

"It inflicted the damage on the other ship. That one's called the *Infidel*."

"Wait a minute," Tambu interrupted. "What is the source of your information? How do you know the *Mongoose* is a pirate ship?"

"I've got a survivor here. Found him hiding in the corridor. He's more than a little hysterical. Keeps babbling that he doesn't want to be hanged. Claims he'll tell us anything or do anything if we don't turn him over to the authorities."

Tambu leaned forward with a new eagerness. The survivor might be able to supply them with the answers to some of the questions they had on how pirates operated.

"Is he the only survivor?" he asked.

"He's the only one on this ship. There were three others who bought it when we chewed 'em up with our slicers. But you ready for this? There are six more on board the *Infidel*."

"What?" Tambu was unable to contain his surprise.

"That's right. A bunch of the crew took a shuttle over to check the *Infidel*'s cargo just before we showed up. One of them is the *Mongoose*'s captain."

Tambu paused to think. On the one hand, the captured pirates could supply them with much-needed information. On the other hand, they outnumbered the *Scorpion*'s crew seven to four. That could be trouble— particularly if they still had their captain to lead them.

"Do you want me to take the shuttle over and check 'em out?" Egor asked, breaking the silence.

"No! Stay where you are for now. I need you there to make sure none of them try to sneak back on board."

Actually, Tambu was afraid the pirates would overpower Egor if he tried to board the *Infidel*, but he didn't want to say that. Egor was so proud of his brawling abilities that he might just take it as a challenge and try it on his own.

"Do you have any way of communicating with the boarding party?" Tambu asked.

"Just a second—I'll check."

There was a brief silence, then Egor spoke again.

"They're using hand communicators, same as us. They're on a different frequency though. I can hold mine next to theirs if you want to talk to them direct."

"Just relay this message to their captain. Tell him to take their shuttle to our ship—alone. I want to talk to him. Let me know when you get confirmation."

Staring at the ships on the viewscreen, Tambu set aside the hailing microphone he had been using to communicate with Egor, then leaned forward to use the ship's intercom speaker.

"Okay, you've heard the plan," he said. "Now here's what I want you to do. Puck, you swing your guns round to cover the *Infidel*. Whitey, stay with the maneuvering controls, but be ready to take over Egor's battery if anything happens with the *Mongoose*. The guns should be set already, but check 'em out just to be sure. I want them set so that all you have to do is hit the firing button. I'll go down to the shuttle docking port to deal with the prisoner. Call me on the intercom if anything strange starts to happen. Any questions?"

"Just the one I asked before," Whitey drawled. "I'm still waiting for an answer."

"I'm sorry—I've forgotten the question." Tambu admitted.

"The question was if we were going to sell the two ships, and if not, why?" Whitey prompted.

"We'll discuss it after I've talked to the *Mongoose*'s captain."

"What's to discuss?" Whitey argued. "What would we do with three ships?"

"We could cover three times as much space, or have one very powerful strike force," Tambu snapped back.

"I should think you'd like that, Whitey. It would mean less fighting and fewer casualties on both sides."

"How do you figure that?"

"If you were running a ship and three heavily armed ships overhauled you and demanded you stand by to be boarded and inspected, would you do it? Or would you try to fight?"

"I see what you mean," Whitey admitted. "I sure wouldn't try to fight three ships. But where would we get crews for the other two ships?"

"That's what I want to talk to the captain of the Mongoose about," Tambu confided.

"You're thinking of hiring them?" Whitey was incredulous. "But they're pirates!"

"Egor to Tambu. Do you read me?"

"Go ahead Egor."

"I've got confirmation for you. The Mongoose's captain is on her way over."

Tambu's eyes jumped to the viewscreen. The shuttle-craft was clearly in sight, steering a straight course for the Scorpion. Then something that Egor had said registered in his mind.

"Egor! Did you say 'her way'?"

"That's right, my friend. It seems your counterpart is female. Young, too, from the sound of her voice. Her name's Ramona. Have fun with your interview."

Tambu grimaced at the leer in Egor's voice, but nonetheless paused to check his appearance in a mirror before heading for the docking hangar.

The captain of the Mongoose was not beautiful, but neither was she repulsive—or even homely. She was small, barely five feet in height, and stocky without really being overweight. A shock of long auburn hair was pulled back into a pony-tail which descended past her waist, combining with her round face to give her an almost schoolgirl appearance.

"Have a seat, Ramona," Tambu said. "We have a lot to talk about."

The girl sank loosely into a chair, casually dangling one leg over its arm.

"You'll forgive my appearance. I was planning to inspect a cargo, not meeting and impressing new people."

She was wearing a form-fitting T-shirt, dark green with a unicorn on it. Her pants were black denim with button-flap pockets on the thighs, and her boots were ankle-high and soft-soled. She was indeed more appropriately dressed for a work crew than for receiving visitors.

"Your appearance does not concern me," Tambu said. "Nor do I find it unpleasant. I do, however, have several questions for you."

"First, I have a question for you," the girl countered. "What do you intend to do with me and my crew?"

"What is usually done with pirates caught in the very act of committing their crimes?" Tambu asked blandly.

"Usually they are turned over to the authorities on the nearest inhabited planet where they are hanged or shot, with or without trial. Occasionally, they are put to death by the ship which captures them." Ramona's eyes met Tambu's squarely. "I might also add that if your plans for us follow those expected patterns, I see no reason why we should answer your questions or cooperate with you in any way."

"And if our plans were to let you go?"

The girl's posture straightened as her air of studied indifference fell away.

"You'd do that? You'd let us take our ship and go?"

"In exchange for information, we'll let you and the crew go. But not the ship. You'll be dropped planetside with no reference to the authorities as to the nature of your business."

"How do I know you aren't lying?" Ramona scowled.

"What's to keep you from getting the information you want, then turning us in anyway?"

"You have no guarantees. You'll just have to trust me. I might point out, however, that if I were lying, I could afford to be a lot more generous with my promises. I could promise you your crew *and* your ship. Instead, I'm being honest. The deal is for your lives—not your ship."

"I guess that makes a certain amount of sense."

"You aren't really in much of a bargaining position," Tambu reminded her.

"Let me ask just one more question. If you give me an honest answer to this one, I'll cooperate."

"What's the question?"

Ramona leaned forward, her expression suddenly fierce. "Who double-crossed us?" she demanded. "Was it someone in my crew?"

"No one double-crossed you. At least, to the best of my knowledge."

"Don't give me that." the girl snapped. "I know the *Infidel* didn't get a distress call out. That means some-one had to tip you about when and where we were going to make our intercept. Otherwise, how did you find us?"

"Blind luck. We had no inside information. In fact, we had no information at all other than the news reports of heavy pirate activity in this region."

"But if you weren't specifically looking for us, how did you know we were pirates?" Ramona challenged.

"We didn't." Tambu smiled. "We had our suspicions as we approached the ships, but that was all. We fired in self-defense when the *Mongoose* turned her guns on us. It wasn't until the surviving crewman confessed that we knew for sure, and even that was uncertain until you confirmed it with your attitude during our interview here."

Ramona was wide-eyed now.

"But—if that's true—" she stammered.

". . . You could have bluffed your way out." Tambu finished the thought for her. "It's a little late for that now, don't you think?"

The girl stared wordlessly for a few moments, then threw back her head and laughed.

"Ramona, the crafty pirate," she declared, shaking her head. "Trapped by blind luck and her own big mouth. Forgive me, but if I don't laugh, I might start crying."

Tambu smiled at her. "Now that you're fully aware of the situation, perhaps you will realize why I'm willing to bargain the way I have. Our aim is to be pirate hunters—sort of a cross between bounty hunters and a police force. It's obvious to me now that we can't simply rely on luck to find our prey. We need to know how pirates think . . . how they operate. That's where you come in. For example, you've implied that you knew in advance where to intercept the *Infidel*. How did you get that information?"

Ramona blinked, then grimaced slightly.

"You really listen close, don't you? Well, on this particular venture, our information came from inside sources."

"Inside sources?" Tambu frowned.

"That's right. I'll tell you my honest opinion. If you're planning to make a living at this, you've got your work cut out for you. The name of the game is information, and it can take years to build up an effective network. How you're going to get informants who will inform on other informants is beyond me."

"Back up a little," Tambu said thoughtfully. "Who are these informants that make up a network?"

"Almost anyone who has information about shipments and an eye for easy money. When I say 'inside sources,' I'm talking about people within the corporate structure of the outfit shipping the cargo out. It could be a shipping clerk, an accountant, or a secretary. Sometimes the information comes directly from upper management when they want to cash in on a little insurance money."

"So you get your information from the shippers themselves?" Tambu asked.

"Some of it," Ramona corrected. "Sometimes it comes from corporations out to sabatoge a rival's shipments. People working at the spaceports themselves are good sources. We even get tips from receiving merchants and corporations who don't want to pay the full price of a shipment."

"I see," Tambu said, pursing his lips. "It sounds as if you have a lot more information than I imagined."

"And you aren't about to let us go until you've pumped it all out of me. Right?" Ramona scowled.

"Actually, I was thinking along different lines. How would you like to come to work for me?"

She held his gaze for a moment, then turned away.

"If you insist," she said flatly. "But you drive a hard bargain. It's extortion, but I don't really have much of a choice, do I?"

"Of course you have a choice!" Tambu thundered, slapping his hand down on the desk hard enough to make it jump with the impact.

Ramona started, taken aback at this sudden display of temper, but Tambu recovered his composure quickly. He rose and began to pace about the room.

"Forgive me," he muttered. "I suppose you have every right to think the way you are. It serves me right for trying to be so cagey instead of laying my cards on the table from the first."

He stopped pacing and perched on the edge of his desk facing her.

"Look," he said carefully, "it's been my intent all along to offer you and your crew positions in my force. I need experienced people—particularly people with experience in space combat—to man my ships. What I

don't need are a bunch of sullen animals who think
they were blackmailed into serving and who will jump
ship or turn on me at the first opportunity. That's why I
was saying I'd let you go instead of turning you over to
the authorities. If you or any of your crew want to sign
on, fine. If not, we'll let them go. Now do we understand
each other?"

Again their eyes met. This time Ramona's expression
was thoughtful, rather than guarded.

"I'll talk to my crew," she said at last. "For my part,
though, the main hesitation isn't money . . . it's position. I worked a long time to get where I am, captaining
my own ship. In all honesty, I'm not sure how content
I'd be working under someone else again. Still, if you let
me go, I'll probably end up crewing again for a while. I
just don't know. I'll have to think about it."

"What if I offered you a position as captain of your
own ship?" Tambu asked.

Hope flashed across the girl's face for a moment.

"I don't want to sound suspicious again," she said
carefully, "but that sounds a little too good to be true.
You capture a pirate ship and crew, then offer to turn
them loose again intact? What's to keep us from going
back to business as normal as soon as you turn your
back?"

"For one thing, your crew would probably be divided
up among the available ships under various command-
ers. For another, we'll probably be operating as a fleet
for a while, which would tend to discourage independent action. There is also the minor detail that I plan to
be on board your ship."

"That sounds to me like I'd be captain in title only."

"Not at all," Tambu assured her. "It's my plan that the
captains under my command have complete autonomy
on their ships, providing, of course, that they stay
within the general guidelines I set forth for them. I
envision my own position to be more of an overall

coordinator for the entire force. I suspect that if all goes
well, that will occupy my time to a point where I will
have neither the time nor the inclination to bother with
the operational details of a single ship—including the
one I'm on."

He uncoiled from his perch and seated himself at his
desk once more.

"My decision to travel on board your ship is to enable
myself to more readily obtain specific information from
you rather than to imply any distrust. That is actually
the answer I should have given you in the first place. I'll
have to trust you, as I'll have to trust all my captains. If I
don't, the force hasn't a hope of success."

Now it was Ramona's turn to rise and pace as she
thought.

"Just how large a fleet are you envisioning?"

"I have no exact figure in mind," Tambu admitted,
"but I expect we will grow well beyond the three ships
we have currently."

"My crew isn't big enough to man even these three
ships," she pointed out.

"I know. We'll have to do some additional recruiting.
I'll want your advice on that, too."

"Aren't you risking trouble using ex-pirates for crew?
I don't mean with mutiny, I'm thinking more about your
reputation."

"My crew might object a bit, at first, but they'll accept
it. If not, they can be replaced."

"I was more concerned with reactions from the
people you'll be dealing with outside the force. I'm not
sure how the merchants will take to being protected by
the very people who were stealing from them not too
long ago."

"We already have a solution to that." Tambu smiled.
"We'll change the names of the ships and crew. That
way no one outside the force has to know anything
about your past. In fact, there's no reason for anyone to

know within the force, either. Your crew doesn't know anything about my crew's background or vice versa. There's no reason they should be told, just as there's no reason we should have to give any background information to the new recruits."

"It'll sure make recruiting a lot easier if the new people don't have to admit to any past indiscretions." Ramona admitted. "Even though God knows what we'll get as a result. It's a little like the old French Foreign Legion."

"It's not a bad parallel. I don't really care what the crew did before they joined, as long as they toe the line once they're under my command."

"Discipline could be a problem," Ramona observed thoughtfully. "You know what would really be effective?"

"What's that?"

"If we made you into a real mystery figure. An omnipresent power with no face." Her voice grew more excited as she warmed to the idea. "You know how superstitious crewmen are. You could become a kind of a boogey-man. It could work against the ships we'll be fighting as well as within our own force."

"And just how would we accomplish that?"

"Hell, we've got a good start already! My crew is already spooked by the way you popped up out of nowhere and blitzed our ship before they could even get a shot off. All we have to do is keep you out of sight, and they'll do the rest. Sound doesn't travel through space, but rumors do. The myth will grow on its own. All we have to do is give it room."

"It won't work." Tambu shook his head. "The one thing I do insist on is meeting each person who's going to serve under me. I have to know who and what I'm commanding if we're going to be effective."

"Do it over a viewscreen. If you keep your sending camera off, you can talk to them and observe them to your heart's content, and all they'll see is a blank screen. As a matter of fact, that would help to build the mystery. Everyone would form their own impression, which means they'll talk about you among themselves trying to get confirmation."

"I'll have to think about it."

"Now is the ideal time to start," Ramona pressured. "Right now, the only ones who know what you look like are your crew and myself. If you wait, then you'll have to try to get cooperation out of the combined crews as well as any new recruits. The sooner you start, the easier it will be."

"But if I'm planning to be on your ship—"

"You can board ahead of the crew. There's a room off my cabin you could take up residence in without anyone being any the wiser. When they talk to you on the viewscreen, they won't know if your signal is coming from somewhere on board or from another ship."

Tambu leaned back and stared at the ceiling as he turned the thought over in his mind.

"It's a good idea," he admitted finally. "Maybe we can give it a try and see how it works. I'll talk to my crew."

"It'll work," Ramona declared triumphantly. "You know, I think we'll work well together. Who knows? If we play our cards right, we might end up ruling the universe."

"Who wants it? Right now I'll settle for eeking out a humble, but substantial, living."

"I know, I know. But when you talk to the new recruits, you might make some veiled references to a secret master plan. It'll help us fill the rosters if they think they're getting in on the ground floor of something big."

"They are," Tambu announced solemnly. "The question is how big—and I figure we won't know the answer to that for a long time yet."

INTERVIEW IV

"Then your original crew was surprised by your plans of expansion?" Erickson asked. Tambu seemed tyrannical, even in his early career.

"I had not deliberately withheld the information from them. The plan had been half-formed in my mind for some time, and I had simply forgotten to tell them about my thinking on the subject. If I had reached a firm decision before encountering the *Mongoose* and its captive, I would have discussed it with them."

"How long had you been thinking about it before you actually implemented the plan?" the reporter pressed.

"I guess it had been in the back of my mind all along," Tambu admitted. "I was always aware of the limitations of a single ship, both in terms of firepower and of coverage."

"Coverage?"

"One ship can be in only one place at a time. If the pirates could figure out where our one ship was, they would know where we weren't, and therefore where it was safe for them to operate. Three ships complicated the problem for them."

"I see," Erickson nodded. "Once you had three ships, though, how did you deploy your original crew—the ones you could be sure of in terms of loyalty?"

"Egor and Whitey were each placed in charge of a ship. I assigned Puck under Whitey."

"Didn't that cause problems with Puck? Giving him a subordinate position while Ramona kept command of her own ship?" the reporter asked, eager for clues of dissention.

"Surprisingly enough, not. I expected him to be much more upset than he actually was. Egor gave me more problems than Puck did."

"What kind of problems did Egor cause?" Erickson pressed.

"It was strange. I had expected problems with Whitey and Puck, but it never occurred to me that Egor would object. Whitey and Puck took the change in stride, but Egor put up an unholy argument. He flatly felt he wasn't qualified for an independent command."

"But you changed his mind, right?" the reporter smiled. "Whitey had commented before on your powers of persuasion."

"Not really," Tambu sighed. "I still maintain Whitey was wrong in attributing superhuman persuasive powers to me, and this is just one example of my failures. I did get Egor to accept a command position, mostly by pointing out there was no one else available with the necessary qualifications whom I trusted."

"What about Puck?"

"Even Egor admitted that Puck was too young for command. Not so much in years, but he lacked maturity. On that basis, Egor accepted command, but he never really agreed with me as to his qualifications."

"So in essence, you forced your will on him?"

Tambu hesitated a moment before answering.

"I suppose you're correct," he said finally. "If that was an error, it's one I paid for a hundredfold afterward. I was constantly receiving complaints, both from Egor and from the other captains as to his shortcomings as a commander. He was probably the least effective captain who ever served under me."

"Why didn't you relieve him of command, then?"

"That is one of those hindsight questions we were speaking of earlier," Tambu admitted. "I've asked myself that a hundred times in the last few years and still haven't come up with a satisfactory answer—mostly because I'm unsure of my own motives during that period. Mostly, I think, it was because of friendship. Egor was my friend, and I gave him command of a ship because I believed in him and his abilities. To take this command away would have been a sign that I no longer believed in him. Balanced against that was my own stubborn pride. I didn't want to admit I had been wrong in my assessment of his abilities, and I sincerely felt that the problems he was encountering were manufactured by him in an effort to prove me wrong. I genuinely believed that once I made it clear that I wasn't going to remove him from command, he would resign himself to the task and solve his own problems. I saw it more as a test of wills than as a sign of incompetence on his part."

"That must have been pretty rough on your friendship."

"It was, particularly as the force continued to grow. As my time was divided across an increasing number of ships, my rapport with my original crew—with my friends—became dangerously thin."

"I can see that," Erickson commented thoughtfully. "Even adding to your fleet by conquest, the number of ships would grow geometrically."

"Even faster than that," Tambu countered. "Few people realize exactly how fast the fleet did grow. You see, not all the new ships came to us as fruits of battle."

CHAPTER FOUR

"You're sure she'll be all right?" Tambu asked again.

"Look, will you relax?" Whitey scolded, her exasperated expression received clearly on the command console viewscreen. "Women have been having babies since prehistoric times. The hospital is more than able to handle any complications that might arise."

"I still don't know why you didn't sign her into the hospital on Carbo when you were there last month," Tambu grumbled. "It's a better facility."

"We aren't talking about a limb transplant," Whitey argued. "It's a childbirth, a simple childbirth. Besides, I tried to talk her into staying on Carbo and she wouldn't do it. Derry can be very strong-willed when she sets her mind to it. What was I supposed to do? Force her to go on shore leave and strand her there?"

"It isn't your fault, Whitey," Tambu sighed. "I know that. It's just this is the first childbirth in the fleet, and I don't want anything to go wrong. I guess I've been taking it out on you. Sorry."

"That's all right," Whitey shrugged. "If you can't

sound off at us, who can you sound off to? Most of the new recruits would faint dead away if you talked to them direct, much less shouted at them."

"It's not quite *that* bad."

"Well, anyway, Pepe's staying with her here on Bastei, so he'll be able to handle any problems that we've overlooked," Whitey continued. "We'll be back in a month to check on things and pick them up if they're ready."

"You're sure they're set on rejoining?" Tambu pressed. "Shipboard is no place to raise a kid."

"I already tried that argument, and it didn't work. Derry was raised on shipboard."

"But that probably wasn't a fighting ship. There's a difference."

"We haven't done any fighting for a long time," Whitey observed. "Anyway, they both want to keep working for us, and I'm not about to stop them. Do you want to overrule me?"

Tambu shook his head, then remembered she couldn't see him.

"No," he said hastily. "It's your ship, and if you're willing to put up with it, I won't interfere."

"Good," Whitey nodded. "Then it's settled."

"She *is* registered at the hospital under her real name, isn't she?" Tambu frowned.

"Yes, she is!" Whitey exclaimed. "And her medical records have been transferred from her home planet. That's what I meant in my original report when I said we were following recommended procedures. *Your* recommended procedures."

"I'm doing it again, aren't I?" Tambu said.

"Yes, you are." Whitey was still annoyed. "Do you get this wound up over everything that happens in the fleet?"

"Not everything," Tambu admitted, "but a fair number of things."

"You can't afford that—not with eight ships under you. If you can't keep some distance between yourself and the minor hassles of running a ship, it'll tear you apart in no time."

"But if I don't keep track of what's going on—" Tambu began, then broke off.

A small red light had begun to blink insistently on his command console accompanied by a soft chime.

"I'll have to sign off now, Whitey," he explained hurriedly, "I've got a 'blinker' emergency coming in."

"What's up?"

"I don't know. It's from the *Dreamer*."

"Puck's ship?" Whitey exclaimed. "He hasn't been in command for a month yet. What kind of trouble can he have gotten into that quick?"

"That's what I'm about to find out," Tambu announced grimly, reaching for the cutoff switch.

"Well, sometime when you get a few minutes, give me a call so we can talk about other things than business." Whitey called desperately. "We never just talk anymore."

"Right," Tambu agreed absently, "I'll do that. Tambu out."

He was hitting buttons as he spoke, switching the communications relays to accept the *Dreamer's* transmission. Whitey's face faded, to be replaced immediately by Puck's worried features.

"Tambu here," he announced, forcing a calm tone into his voice. "What's the problem, Puck?"

"I'm—I'm not sure it's a problem," Puck stammered in return.

"Well, then, why don't you just tell me why you put in a priority call?" Tambu suggested patiently.

"We've got a pirate ship here. It came up out of nowhere and caught us with our sails out."

"How big a ship?"

"About twice our size. And armed to the teeth. If it opened fire, we wouldn't have a chance."

"Then I'd say you have a problem," Tambu announced grimly. "I take it from your comments that so far it hasn't fired on you?"

"That's right. It's just sitting out there watching us. We've got its captain on the horn, and he says he wants to talk to you."

"To me? About what?"

"He won't say, but he says if you aren't on board our ship, we should relay his transmission to you."

"All right, patch him through."

"Will do," Puck acknowledged. "Should we try to get our sails in while you're talking?"

"Negative. If he wants to talk, let's hear what he has to say before you try anything. Monitor the conversation, though, and keep your weapons manned. If you hear me say my name—the one I was using when we first met—open fire and try to knock him out before he returns fire."

"Got it," Puck nodded vigorously. "Oh, Tambu, one more thing you should know. The captain says his name is Blackjack. I think he's the same one you met back on Trepec."

"I see. Very well, patch him through."

There was a few moments' pause. Then Puck's face faded and was replaced by the impatient countenance of Blackjack. Tambu watched in silence for several moments as the man fidgeted.

"You wanted to speak with me?" he said at last.

Blackjack started, then squinted at the screen as his hands went to the control dials.

"Excuse me," he apologized hastily. "There must be an equipment malfunction. I'm not receiving a picture. If I had known you were standing by—"

"It is not an equipment malfunction," Tambu interrupted. "For security reasons, my picture is never transmitted."

"Oh," Blackjack blinked. "Of course. A very sound policy."

Tambu smiled in wry amusement. As incredible as it seemed, Blackjack hadn't recognized his voice. The difference between the swaggering bully he had met on Trepe and the servile figure on the screen was ludicrous.

"You said you wanted to speak with me?" he asked levelly. "My time *is* limited."

Blackjack licked his lips nervously. "Well, sir, we've heard that you're forming a peacekeeping force and were accepting members who were . . . that is, regardless of their past records."

"That is correct. And in answer to your unasked question, some of our crews have been pirates in the past."

Blackjack smiled. "Good, because we'd like to join up. I mean, we'd like to become a part of your force, if that's possible."

Tambu raised his eyebrows in surprise. This was a turn of events he hadn't anticipated.

"I know this is irregular," Blackjack continued hastily, misinterpreting the silence. "But if you could just supply us with a few details as to what you're expecting—"

"Why?" Tambu interrupted.

Anger flashed momentarily in Blackjack's eyes, and his posture stiffened. Then he regained his smile.

"I know it's an annoyance, but it's been hard getting a line on your operations. We figured maybe if we went right to the source—"

"I meant why do you want to join. I was under the impression you had a lucrative business of your own going."

"You've heard of me?" Blackjack seemed both surprised and flattered.

"We have our sources," Tambu countered, smiling to himself. "It was my belief that you were a diehard loner. I fully expected that if our courses crossed, that you'd be taken dead or not at all. As such, I'm quite curious about your sudden change of heart."

"Well, the business has never been all that stable, and it's been getting rougher lately. You should know that. You're one of the reasons things have been going bad."

"We have had some modest success."

"It was shaky enough when things were one-on-one and every ship for itself. But now that we're up against ships working together in teams or packs—well, let's say the odds are getting pretty high against us."

"Have you thought of quitting?" Tambu suggested.

"We talked it over, the crew and me, but none of us were wild about finding work planetside, and cargo hauling seems awfully dull after the life we've been living."

"Besides, it doesn't pay as well," Tambu observed dryly.

"Exactly. Well, anyway, we decided to go with the old saying . . . you know, 'if you can't lick 'em, join 'em.' So here we are. What do you say?"

"It still sounds like a rather abrupt change of face to me. I'm surprised your crew isn't more averse to changing sides this way."

Blackjack shrugged. "Cops or robbers, the game's the same on both sides of the fence. The big difference is that playing it your way, we can mix with polite company."

"Well, we haven't exactly been swamped with invitations to society balls," Tambu countered. "And I'd like to think there are a few differences between the cops and the robbers. The main one that comes to mind is discipline. If you join the fleet, you play by my rules. You'll be allowed to run your ship your way, but the final decisions are mine. No solo jaunts or independent action."

"I know that. That's the price we pay for joining a group. Between you and me, though, in a lot of ways, it's a plus, not a minus. I don't mind at all passing the buck on some of the rougher decisions."

"Exactly what are you expecting to get out of this?"

"You don't buy the 'noble cause' bit, eh?" Blackjack grimaced.

"Let's say I have limited faith in it. I think the best business relationships exist when both sides benefit from the arrangement. If you join, I get another ship complete with a trained crew. Now what are you seeing that you'll get out of this?"

"Support. Both military and financial. Not only do we have allies we can call on if we get our ass in a sling, by sharing profits and losses, we stabilize our cash flow."

"Now that's the kind of selfish answer I can relate to. For the first time, Blackjack, I'm starting to believe you."

Blackjack sighed. "Now that that's settled, where do we go from here? Do we have to actually fight with your ship here, or can we just surrender and save wear and tear on everybody?"

"I think we can dispense with that in this case. Instead, why don't you have your ship tag along with the *Dreamer* for awhile. I'll instruct the captain to fill you in on our procedures and fleet policies. Then we can talk again."

"Fine by me." Blackjack smiled. "Anything else, boss?"

"Yes, start organizing the personnel records for your crew. I'll want to go over them with you next time we talk."

"Why?" Blackjack asked suspiciously. "I thought selection and assignment of the crew was my responsibility."

"It is," Tambu soothed. "I just like to be familiar with the individuals serving under me."

'All right. It might take awhile, though. I was never big on recordkeeping."

"I'm particularly curious about two of your crew," Tambu commented, unable to resist the jibe. "One of them is a short-haired blonde in her late twenties; the other is a boy in his mid-teens, Spanish-looking. I think you know who I mean."

Blackjack was visibly unsettled by the request.

"You weren't kidding when you said you had your sources, were you?" he said wonderingly.

"No, I wasn't. Tambu out."

He waited until Blackjack's face was gone, then leaned into his console once more.

"Are you still there, Puck?" he asked.

"Didn't miss a word," Puck replied, his features materializing on the screen.

"Good," Tambu nodded. "Try to get invited on board Blackjack's ship—and take a few extra people with you. I want a report from you on their armament and personnel to check against Blackjack's data. Can do?"

"Affirmative, boss."

"Keep me posted, then. Tambu out."

For a few minutes, Tambu leaned back in his chair smiling to himself. He considered calling Whitey, but rejected the thought. The board was clear, and his eyes hurt from staring at the screen for so many hours.

On an impulse, he rose and moved to the door of his cabin, activating the small intercom set into the wall. Hearing no conversation in the adjoining cabin, he depressed the button by the volume knob.

For long moments he waited, knowing that Ramona might not notice the small light glowing on her console even if she were in her cabin.

"Yes, boss?" Her voice came through the intercom at last.

"Can you come in here for a moment? Nothing important. I just want to talk to a live person for a while."

"Sure. Coming through."

He reached down and unlocked his side of the door, and a moment later heard the click as she unlocked her side.

"Care for some wine?" he offered as she entered the cabin. "I opened a half-bottle a couple hours back and haven't gotten around to drinking more than a glass."

"Only if you'll join me," she smiled. "It's silly, but my

mother always told me a lady never drinks alone."

"Why not?" he smiled gesturing at the blank call-board. "The fleet seems to be handling its own problems for a change."

He draped himself over a chair and waited while Ramona poured two glasses of wine. Passing one to him, she pulled up another seat and sank into it, curling her legs up under her.

"You seem to be in an exceptionally good mood tonight," she observed, cocking her head to one side. "Good news on the board?"

"Not really," he frowned. "Just no bad news. There was one funny incident, though."

"Tell me about it."

"Well, I just got done talking with Blackjack. You remember I told you about him? The pirate we ran into on Trepec? The one who was going to get even with us?"

"I remember," Ramona nodded, sipping her wine. "What did he want?"

"He wanted to join the fleet, but that's not what tickled me. The funny part was that he didn't recognize me—my voice, that is. I wonder how he'd react if he knew the Tambu he was dealing with in such humble tones was the same man who took his gun away from him in a bar on Trepec?"

"That's it? That was your laugh of the day?"

"Well, I suppose it doesn't sound like much," Tambu admitted, crestfallen. "You would have had to have been there."

"I just don't think it's all that surprising that he didn't recognize you. You've changed a lot, you know."

"How so?"

"I didn't mean that as a criticism. It's just that since you've been coordinating things for several ships instead of one, you've taken on different mannerisms. Your voice has a no-nonsense ring of command to it that wasn't there when we first met."

"I haven't been aware of any changes," he protested.

"You're too close to see it," she pointed out. "But you're taking to command like a duck takes to water. You may have started out playing a role, but now you're it. You're the boss, the chief, the old man. There's a distance between you and everyone else, and it shows in how you talk."

"You mean that now, as we're talking here, I'm putting on airs?" he challenged.

"Not so much now when we're in the same room," Ramona conceded. "But when you're talking to me over the viewscreen, I can feel it. And it isn't putting on airs—it's just a clear knowledge of who orders and who follows."

"You make me sound awfully dictatorial."

"It isn't overt," Ramona insisted. "But there's no doubt in anyone's mind that there's an iron hand in that velvet glove. Nobody ever forgets you've done what no one else even thought of trying—building a united fleet from a bunch of individual ships."

"I'll have to think about that," Tambu sighed thoughtfully. "I thought I was just doing what had to be done to keep the fleet together."

"Did you let Blackjack join?" Ramona asked.

"Tentatively. It may be a mistake. I can't help but wonder how he'll act once he's operating on his own."

"It's my bet he'll be a model captain," Ramona stated. "In case you haven't noticed, the newer the ship, the closer they toe the line. The stronger the fleet gets, the less any individual ship wants to cross you."

"I'd rather have respect and loyalty than fear," Tambu stated flatly.

"You're going to get all three," Ramona insisted. "You're becoming a power, and that tends to polarize people's reactions. Some will love and respect you; others will migrate toward hate and fear."

"That's a bit too much for me in one evening." Tambu rose and stretched. "I'm going to get some sleep while I can. I still maintain I'm just doing my job."

"I'm not so sure it's always going to be that simple," Ramona retorted, uncoiling and starting for the door. "Remember, even now, the only one defining your job is you!"

INTERVIEW V

Erickson took advantage of the recess to inspect the room more closely. His confidence had grown until now he was more relaxed than at the beginning of the interview. Of particular interest to him was the collection of books which adorned the walls.

Much to his surprise, the titles were mostly of an economic or philosophical nature. For some reason, he had been expecting the main thrust of the literature to be military history. Like Tambu, the library was proving to be inconsistent with his preconceived notions.

He was about to take a volume down for closer inspection when Tambu's voice came over the console's speaker once more.

"I'm ready to continue now, Mr. Erickson. Please forgive the interruption."

"It's quite all right," the reporter waved, taking his seat once more. "I must confess, however, that it had somehow never occurred to me that the feared Tambu would occasionally have to go to the bathroom like anyone else."

"It's a common misconception surrounding public figures," Tambu said. "When the average person thinks of an actor, a politician, or an athlete, they always view them within the context of their specialty. The thought that they must occasionally perform some very ordinary tasks such as shining shoes or doing the laundry never enters into the picture."

"That's true," Erickson admitted. "I guess it's just a matter of ego-defense."

"Ego-defense? I don't believe I understand your point."

"Well, when an ordinary Joe looks at a celebrity, there's always one question in the back of his mind: 'What has he got that I don't?' If he lets himself view the celebrity as just another person, it means he must see himself as inferior. Since most people strive to see themselves as above average, they reject the thought that an ordinary person can achieve that much more success given the same materials to work with. As a result, rather than accept an inferior self-image, they are more comfortable projecting the celebrity into superhuman status. The view then is: 'I'm above average, but they're special! I don't have to compare myself with them because they're another species completely.' As I said, it's self-defense—or rather ego-defense."

"An interesting concept," Tambu commented after a moment's pause. "While I've observed the phenomenon, that is one interpretation I had never considered. Perhaps we can discuss it further later, if I have any extra time left at the end of our interview."

"I somehow doubt that." Erickson smiled. "Just what we've covered so far has raised so many questions in my mind that I'm sure the interview will last as long as time allows."

"In that case, we should probably proceed," Tambu said. "What questions do you have so far?"

"One question I've been asking in various ways since the beginning of the interview still sticks in my mind.

You've answered it indirectly with your narrative, but I'd still like a simple 'yes or no' response. When you began organizing your force, did you think you were doing the right thing? Did you see your force as the good guys?"

"The simple answer is 'yes'!" Tambu replied. "The actual answer is far more complex. I was hoping you could see that by now."

"The complexity escapes me. It seems a very straightforward question."

"It becomes complex when I add that what we were doing was right in my own mind, not just at the beginning, but to this very day. However, I am aware that I do not have an exclusive patent on truth. What's right in my mind is not necessarily right in the minds of others. From there it's a matter of who you believe or which philosophy you embrace."

"But facts are facts," the reporter argued impatiently.

"Very well," Tambu sighed. "The facts are that we were successful. We waged war against the pirates infesting the trade and made enough of a dent in their numbers that their activity all but ceased. That is a fact which can be confirmed through your own newspaper's files. By examining our record you can see we were a law-enforcing group."

"Enforcing whose law?" Erickson jibed. "Yours?"

"You're defeating your own arguments, Mr. Erickson. You're attempting to interpret the facts. The factual response to your question, however, is that yes, we were enforcing my laws. There were no interstellar laws until I formulated them with my fleet. To judge beyond that requires interpretation. Was I bringing law and order to the previously lawless starlanes? Or was I an opportunistic bandit taking advantage of that lawless state?"

"I'm beginning to see your point," the reporter admitted hesitantly. "But what happened next? What happened once you gained the upper hand over the pirates?"

"Then," Tambu reminisced, "we began to encounter the same problem which has confronted peacetime armies since the dawn of time."

CHAPTER FIVE

"There's no sign of them at the other two inhabited planets in this system either. We've checked with instruments and confirmed with firsthand investigation. They aren't here."

Tambu slouched in his chair studying the angry face of the *Candy Cane*'s captain on the viewscreen before him. He was as concerned over the mental state of the captain as he was about the unfortunate turn of events being reported.

"Have you checked planetside?"

"On all three planets," the captain confirmed. "There hasn't been a ship in this system in weeks. With your permission, I'd like to find the lying bastard who sold us this information and get our money back—with interest!"

Tambu grimaced at the suggestion, confident the captain could not see his expression. He had several unconfirmed reports on the captain of the *Candy Cane*, all regarding unnecessary brutality. The last thing he

wanted to do was to give the man carte blanche to lean
on one of their informants.

"Have you checked the uninhabited planets?" he
asked, stalling for time.

The expression of anger on the captain's face gave
way to one of uneasiness.

"We've run an instrument check, but not a firsthand
confirmation," he admitted. "I figured if the Chameleon
was putting in for R and R and supplies they'd be at one
of the inhabited planets. I mean, there's no point in
giving your crew shore leave on a hunk of barren rock.
Shall I go ahead and check out the other planets?"

Tambu had reached his decision as the captain spoke.

"No, that won't be necessary. I want you to hold firm
at that system for a while, though. Wait at least a week
and see if our target pops up. He might just be running
late."

The captain grimaced, then remembered that Tambu
could still see him and rearranged his features into a
forced smile.

"Hold position for a week," he repeated. "Affirmative."

"For the record," Tambu said casually, "What are you
figuring as your modus operandi for that week?"

It was an unfair question. The captain had just gotten
his orders, and it was obvious he couldn't have a set
plan of action in mind yet. Still, Tambu expected his
captains to be able to be able to think on their feet.
Besides, he hadn't liked the way the captain reacted
when receiving his orders.

"Um . . ." the captain began, licking his lips nervously, "we'll leave a crewman at each spaceport on the
three inhabited planets, then take up position close
enough to the furthest uninhabited planet that it will
screen our position. If the target ship shows up, our
watchers can contact us by closed communicator and
we'll move in."

Tambu let the captain suffer in silence for a full minute before he answered.

"That plan seems adequate. How do you intend to select which crewmen are to serve as watchers?"

"On the merit system," the captain replied promptly, his confidence apparently bolstered by the acceptance of his plan. "An all-expense-paid week planetside is a pretty nice plum. I figure it should go to my pest performers."

"That also means your best performers will be off-ship when you take on the target vessel," Tambu commented pointedly.

The captain's face fell at the admonishment, but Tambu continued.

"It's good to hear that. I wish more of my captains had that kind of faith in their crews instead of letting a few key crewmembers handle all the dirty work."

"I—Thank you, sir," the captain gulped.

"One suggestion, though," Tambu drawled, smiling at the captain's discomfort. "You might choose one of the watchers by random draw, then rig it so one of your newer crewmembers wins. Send someone with a bit of experience along to be sure he stays out of trouble, but make it clear it's the new man's assignment. Also, I think you should put all the watchers on a budget just to make sure they don't get carried away with their spending. They're there to do a job, not to go on a binge."

"Yes, sir."

"And announce to the crew that if you nail the target, there will be a week's shore leave at a planet of your choice."

"Yes, sir. Thank you." The captain was smiling now.

"Tambu out."

Tambu didn't smile as he clicked off the viewscreen. He took no pleasure or pride in dealing with situations such as this. They were all too commonplace now, more the rule than the exception.

Swiveling his chair away from the communications console, he faced his desk once again. The jumble of papers and notepads stared back at him in unswerving accusation. He realized that he viewed the work before him with neither enthusiasm nor distaste. He was too tired to muster any reaction.

He briefly considered the possibility of a short nap, but rejected the thought. He would double-check these figures once more, then take a break. With an involuntary sigh, he reached for a pencil.

Behind him, the communications console chimed softly, signaling an incoming call.

Tambu turned from his desk and reached for the switch to activate the mechanism. His eye fell on the call board, and he hesitated.

The incoming call was being relayed through several ships. This was the normal precaution taken to hide his exact location. The ship originating the call was the *Scorpion*. Egor!

Tambu scowled at the board, his hand poised over the activator switch. For a moment, he was tempted to ignore the call. Then the console chimed again, and he threw the switch. As long as Egor was one of his captains, he would be afforded the same prompt attention as any other captain, no matter how annoying it was.

"Yes, Egor?" Tambu asked, forcing his voice into a neutral tone.

"Saladin says you approved the transfer of Jocko from the *Scorpion* to the *Ramses*." Egor's snarl exploded over the speaker even before his face blinked into focus.

"That is correct," Tambu replied levelly.

"Did you know Jocko is the second-best navigator in my crew?" Egor's face was on the screen now, and his expression matched his voice.

"I knew it," Tambu admitted without apology.

"Why wasn't I consulted?" Egor demanded. "Doesn't my say matter for anything anymore?"

As Egor spoke, the door of Tambu's office opened a crack, and Ramona's head appeared. She cocked an eyebrow in silent question, and he waved her inside.

"In this case, Egor, your opinion was already known," Tambu explained patiently. "You had already turned down Jocko's transfer request. That's why he came to me directly."

"So you just countermanded my authority," Egor scowled. "Without even bothering to ask my reasons."

"As Jocko explained it to me, he was either going to transfer or leave the force." Tambu's voice had an edge to it now. "Either way, the *Scorpion* was going to lose him. At least this way he's still in the force. As you pointed out, he's a good navigator."

"I still don't think you should have let him blackmail you." Egor was sullen now.

"What are we supposed to do? Chain him to his bunk?" Tambu's annoyance was beginning to show. "We can't hold people against their will. Even if we could, I wouldn't. I want ships crewed by free men, not slaves."

"Well, I still think you should have talked to me," Egor grumbled.

"I was going to, Egor," Tambu apologized. "But things have been so hectic at this end I haven't had time."

"That's been happening a lot lately," Egor complained bitterly. "I always seem to be at the end of your priority list. You can find time for everybody but your old friends."

"Damn it, Egor," Tambu snapped. "I spend more time talking to you than with any three of my other captains."

"Which is less than a tenth of the time you used to have for me! Of course, now that you're a big shot, I can't expect you to waste your precious time on my problems."

Tambu drew a long breath before responding.

"Look, Egor," he said gently. "Speaking for a moment as an old friend, you might ease up a little on your crew. If you did, a lot of the problems you're having would never arise."

"Don't tell me how to run my ship! I'm allowed to do things my way as long as it doesn't go against the rules. You just worry about the fleet and keep your bloody hands off my ship!"

"*Captain* Egor," Tambu replied coldly. "If you wish to retain full responsibility for the running of your ship, I suggest that you be man enough to begin taking full responsibility for solving your own problems instead of whining for me to clean up your messes. Tambu out!"

"But—"

Tambu smashed his fist down on the activator switch, cutting off Egor's response.

A touch at his shoulder made him jump. He had forgotten that Ramona was in the room.

"I'm sorry, Ramona," he sighed, sinking back in his chair. "I didn't think things were going to get that hot."

"How many times do I have to tell you," she said gently, standing behind him to massage his neck and shoulders, "it's Ratso now, not Ramona. You should follow your own rules."

"I don't like the name Ratso," he complained. "I'll use it in formal communications, but privately you'll always be Ramona to me."

"Other crewmen have picked names you don't like, but you use them," she teased.

"I don't sleep with the other members of the force! I just can't accept the idea of sharing a bed with someone called Ratso."

They had drifted into an affair after several months of working together. What began as a shared moment of passion had grown into a gentle and tender partnership which neither of them questioned.

"When are you going to do something about Egor?" she asked absently.

"Egor's one of our oldest captains. His seniority gives him certain considerations."

"He's a braggart and a bully. Everyone in the fleet knows that."

"He has an irritating manner," Tambu admitted, "but he's a good man. You've just got to know him before you can see through his bluster."

"If so, you must be the only one who can do it. The other captains are wondering why you don't boot him out, or at least pull his command."

"Look, just drop it, huh?" Tambu winced. "Egor is my problem, so it's up to me to come up with a solution. Okay?"

"Sure," she shrugged. "Didn't mean to get on your back. Did you get any sleep at all last night?"

"Not much," he sighed, relaxing under her skillful hands. "It seems everyone has decided that the easiest time to get through to me is the middle of the night. Then again, there's all this."

He gestured at the papers on his desk.

"What is all that, anyway?" Ramona asked. "You've been working on it nonstop for a couple of weeks now."

"I've been going over the books checking our cash flow," he explained. "I've got to check the numbers again, but if the preliminary figures hold true, we're going to be out of business by the end of the year."

"Are things that bad?"

"Actually, things are that good." Tambu laughed bitterly. "We're suffering from being too successful. There are only so many pirates for us to capture, and the ones that are left are giving us wide berth. We've been paying the crews out of the treasury for nearly a year now, and we aren't making enough in salvage and reward money to replenish it. In short, our expenses have remained constant while our income has gone down. We're in trouble."

"Actually, our expenses have gone up," Ramona

commented thoughtfully. "Now that we're up to twenty-four ships . . ."

"Twenty-eight."

"Twenty-eight?" she echoed. "Where did the other four ships come from?"

"One captured, three joined." he recited mechanically.

"Joined?" Ramona frowned. "But you can't keep letting new ships into the fleet."

"I thought you were the one who argued for that in the first place," Tambu teased. "Most of the ships in the fleet are joiners."

"At first, yes. But we can't keep expanding if we're running out of money and targets."

"We need the extra ships and the contacts."

"But that just means more . . ." She broke off and looked at him suspiciously. "You've got a plan, don't you? You always have a plan."

"Not always, but most of the time."

"Well, come on," she prodded, poking him in the ribs. "What is it?"

"Nothing much," he said casually. "Just a complete reformating of our force."

He paused, as if expecting her to respond enthusiastically. Instead, she gnawed her lip.

"How complete?" she asked warily.

"Well, so far we've been living on rewards and salvage. The books show the flaw in that system—no fighting, no loot. I figure we're ready to move onto the next locial stage."

"And that would be. . . ?"

"That we hire ourselves out as a peacekeeping force. That way we get paid whether there's fighting or not. In fact the less fighting there is, the more we should be paid."

"How do you figure that?"

"Easy," he smiled. "in theory, we'll be paid to keep

the trade routes free of pirates. If we botch the job and somebody loses a shipment, we might have to refund part of our fee; but as long as things go smoothly, we get full payment."

"Full payment from who? Refund our fee to who?" Ramona pressed. "Just who are you expecting to foot the bill for all this?"

"The ones who are benefiting from our services. The corporations and the merchants. I still have to figure out how to spread the cost around proportionately but I figure it should be a small percentage of the value of each shipment, to be paid equally by the shipper and the receiver."

"What if they won't pay?" Ramona asked pointedly. "So far they've been getting the service for free."

"If they won't pay, we take our ships away and guard the systems that will pay. When the word gets around that a system is unguarded, the pirates will move in again. Sooner or later, the systems will come around to seeing it our way and will ante up."

"I don't know. It sounds a little too good to be true. I'd like to hear what a couple of the other captains have to say about this."

"I can go you one better than that. You'll have a chance to hear what all the captains have to say about it."

"How so?"

"I'm planning to have a mass meeting of the entire fleet, specifically to get the captains all in one place so I can sell this idea to them all at once. It's a little too big for a unilateral decision."

"And if they don't agree with you?"

"Then I'll resign and let someone else take a shot at running the show." Tambu's tone was light, but his sagging shoulders betrayed the depth of his emotion. "I see it as our only hope for survival, but I can't lead if no one will follow."

"Then it's a unilateral decision," Ramona stated flatly. "No one's going to buck you if you feel that strongly about it."

"Don't be so sure. Sometimes I think some of the captains automatically take the opposite position I do just to be ornery."

"I *am* sure," Ramona insisted. "And if you don't realize what's going on, it's about time you took another look at things. Sure the captains argue with you, because they know you respect people who think for themselves and speak their minds. You tell each person who signs on this force that you won't tolerate 'yesmen,' and they take it to heart. They'll argue because you tell 'em to, but don't kid yourself into thinking they'll go against you on anything big. You're Tambu, and you call the shots in this outfit. They wouldn't have it any other way."

Tambu stared at the blank viewscreen, avoiding her eyes as he thought.

"I don't know," he sighed finally. "I hope you're wrong, but a lot of what you're saying fits what's been going on. You know what they say about absolute power corrupting absolutely? Well, I'm no different from anybody else. It scares me to think what I'd be like if I let myself believe I've got total control over the force. I mean, even with the ships we have now, without any further expansion, we're strong enough to seize and hold a half dozen systems—not planets, *systems*. We could do it, and there's not a force in the universe that could stop us."

"You know, I hadn't thought about it, but you're right." Ramona admitted.

"But, you see, that's what bothers me," Tambu pressed earnestly. "I *do* think about those things. That's what scares me. Do you know the thing that makes me suppress the thoughts? I don't think the force would go along with it. The fact that it's immoral or wrong doesn't

enter my mind, just that I don't think the force would
back me. I think they'd finally be convinced I'd lost my
mind and toss me out on my ear. Maybe I shouldn't say
it, but I like being Tambu. With all the arguments and
the lost sleep, I *like* running the force."

"I know," Ramona soothed, rubbing his shoulders
again. "I'd hate to think you were putting up with all
this if you didn't like it. As you say, you're no different
than anybody else. There's a need inside everybody to
make an impact on society or history . . . to make a
difference. Where you're special is that you can do it.
How many people could run this force, much less build
it? You have something—call it charisma or whatever,
but people trust you and believe in you. They believe
that you'll make that difference in history, and if they
follow you, they'll be a part of it. They believe that in
serving under you, they'll go further than they ever
would on their own, and they're right. Would Egor or
Puck ever command a ship of their own if you hadn't
given them the opportunity? You talk about the force.
You *are* the force. The captains and their crews are loyal
to *you*, not the force. They tolerate each other because
you order it, but you're the glue that holds the whole
thing together."

"That's the other reason I'm calling for a mass meeting," Tambu muttered darkly. "I want the captains to
start interacting more, not just tolerating each other. I'm
betting that once they're all together, talking and sharing drinks, they'll find out that their problems are not
unique or individual, but shared by every other captain
in the fleet. With any luck, friendships will spring up
and they'll start calling each other for answers instead
of coming to me all the time. I'll wait until the end of the
meeting to see if anyone else suggests making the meeting an annual affair—and if no one does, I'll suggest it
myself."

"I don't know if you're overestimating the force or

underestimating them," Ramona commented, shaking her head. "But it's not going to work."

"Thanks. I always appreciate a little support for my plans."

"Oh, the meeting will go okay, but I don't think it will accomplish what you want it to—your hidden motive, I mean."

"Hidden motive?" Tambu frowned.

"You should listen to yourself as closely as you listen to the captains," Ramona laughed. "What you've been saying is that if the captains start talking to each other and find answers among themselves, then maybe it will ease your status as answer man, that it will give you a chance to ease down off your pedestal. What you're overlooking is that you're still instigating it, and the captains will see that. None of them thought of getting together to help each other until you ordered it, just like no one thought of assembling a space fleet until you did it. It may get you off the spot for specific questions and issues, but you'll still be Number One who can do things no one else even thinks of."

"I don't know. I'm too tired to think straight anymore. Maybe it will seem clearer tomorrow."

"How tired are you?" Ramona drawled, pressing herself against him.

"Well . . ." Tambu mused with mock solemnity, "I was thinking of going to bed."

They kissed and moved toward the bed with their arms around each other's waists.

The communications console chimed softly.

Ramona groaned dramatically, and Tambu swore under his breath.

"I'll try to keep this short," he promised.

A glance at the call board identified the call as coming from the Raven. Whitey!

"Yes, Whitey?" he asked flipping on the activator switch.

As Whitey's face swam into focus, he noted there were circles of fatigue under her eyes.

"Sorry to call you so late," she apologized, "but I just finished a brainstorming session with my crew and wanted to get a hunk of uninterrupted time with you."

"What's the problem?"

"Well, we just finished investigating a complaint by some of the planetside folk that a couple of our boys busted up a bar and put two people in the hospital."

"Which crewmen?"

"That's the whole point. When we checked, it turned out that it wasn't our crew at all. A couple of planetside toughs were throwing their weight around and saying they were Tambu's men so they could get away with it. We've had the authorities go through our crew roster, and the witnesses confirmed it wasn't any of our crew; but in the meantime the pilot of our shuttle got jumped at the spaceport and was beaten pretty badly."

"That's unfortunate, but I don't see what I can do about it."

"There's nothing you can do about this specific incident," Whitey agreed. "but the crew came up with an idea that could affect the whole fleet. They say they're tired of taking the blame for things other people do posing as Tambu's men. They suggested we adopt an emblem or something that could be worn by each crew member when they went planetside so that folks would know who they are. We're going to try it for the *Raven's* crew, but you might want to consider doing it with the whole fleet."

"What kind of emblem?" Tambu queried.

"We haven't decided yet," Whitey admitted. "But we're thinking in terms of a belt or an armband, something like that."

"How are you going to keep those same toughs from making their own copies?" Tambu frowned.

"I'll tell you one thing," Whitey grinned. "If they do, I

wouldn't want to be in their shoes if any of my crew
caught them."

"That's not good enough," Tambu insisted. "Tell you
what; call the main spokesmen for your crew up to your
cabin and let's kick this around a little more."

Insulated by the intricacies of this new problem, he
never heard Ramona as she quietly let herself out of his
cabin.

INTERVIEW VI

"I assume the captains approved your plan?" Erickson asked.

"Unanimously. In hindsight, it wasn't surprising. It was either that or disband."

"So you began offering the services of your fleet to the planets on a retainer basis?" the reporter prompted.

"That is correct. And the key word there is 'offered.' When you stop to think about it, it was a good deal for the planets. We had built, armed, and organized the fleet at our own expense. All we were asking them to do was contribute toward maintaining it."

"Yet you encountered resistance to your offer," Erickson recalled. "Didn't that surprise you?"

"Yes and no. We knew from the onset that not everyone would want to contribute. There's an old medical saying which states 'An ounce of prevention is worth a pound of cure.' The anticipated problem was convincing a healthy patient that he needed an ounce of prevention, however reasonably priced it might be."

"Perhaps they thought they were being asked to pay for a pound of prevention where an ounce would suffice."

"I would believe that if they had haggled about the price," Tambu said pointedly. "However, what we encountered was flat refusal. In essence, the planets wanted to reap the benefits of our work without paying a cent."

"They did pay reward money when you destroyed the pirate ships," the reporter reminded him gently.

"The actual fighting was only a fraction of our work," Tambu argued. "If a pirate chose to run or even avoid a planet completely rather than tangle with our ships, we got nothing even though we had effectively performed a service."

"But in that situation your ship hadn't actually done anything," Erickson countered.

"Are your planetside police paid by the arrest? Part of the value of a uniformed patrolman is as a deterrent. Their job is as much to prevent crimes as it is to solve them."

"I take it the planets weren't swayed by your arguments?"

"Some were," Tambu said, calming slightly. "I tend to overgeneralize when I refer to the planetside resistance. Many planets did subscribe to our service, but there were few enough that in my eyes they had to pay an inflated rate. As such we were continually approaching and reapproaching the other planets to subscribe, in an effort to reduce the costs to the individual planet."

"That sounds awfully considerate," Erickson observed, not really believing it.

"Only partially," Tambu admitted. "The other side of the coin was that we were afraid if we didn't find a way to spread our fees more, that the subscribing planets would decide they were paying too much and withdraw from our roster."

"While you're speaking candidly," the reporter

prodded, "I couldn't help but notice a note of bitterness in your voice when you spoke about the resisting planets. How deep did the emotions run in your fleet over that initial resistance?"

"There were two kinds of bitterness prevalent in the fleet at that time. The first was over the injustice of the refusals. We lost numerous ships in our campaigns against the pirates—ships with friends and comrades on board. It did not sit well with us to be told by the planets that we hadn't really done anything or risked anything. That was a bitterness we had anticipated, and as such kept under control."

"And the other kind?" Erickson urged.

"The other kind was over the method of the refusals. As I mentioned earlier, we hadn't expected all the planets to agree to our proposal. Though we felt our position was reasonable and justified, we held no grudge against an opinion to the contrary. What did surprise us was the venom with which our offer was refused. While most of our crews owned no allegiance or loyalty to the planets, neither did they harbor any ill-will—that is, until they encountered the warm greeting some of the planets had prepared for anyone off a Tambu ship."

CHAPTER SIX

Tambu bent forward over his console and pressed his palms over his ears, unsuccessfully attempting to block out the babble of voices gushing from the viewscreen's speaker. Failing that, he drew a breath to speak angrily, then reconsidered. Almost of its own volition, his hand flipped a switch and the scene on the viewscreen changed, now displaying the space outside his ship.

Looking at the stars was becoming a habit with him, a ploy he relied on more and more to put his own problems in perspective. This time, however, the stars were partially obscured, upstaged by the vast armada of ships gathered here. Militarily, it was the strongest force in the universe, boasting more fighting ships than any planet—than any system could field. Many people outside the force feared its power. They were all too aware of the potential danger of this many ships united under a common cause.

United! Tambu smiled wryly. Those people would worry less if they had the vaguest idea of what actually went on within the fleet. The babble of voices rose in volume. Tambu sighed and readjusted the screen back to its original display.

It was a large room, one of the cargo holds of the *Raven*. Chairs had been packed in wall-to-wall to provide seating, but at the moment most of the room's occupants were on their feet shouting and arguing with each other.

Tambu watched for a moment, then shook his head and leaned toward the microphone.

"I will entertain a motion to gas the room," he announced firmly.

Heads snapped around and arguments died in midsentence at the sound of his voice. Silence spread through the crowd like a wave, leaving shocked and wary stares in its wake.

"Now that I have your undivided attention, allow me to remind you of our situation. Each of you is a captain of a ship under my command. You are here to represent your ship's interests in discussions of the fleet's policies and procedures, as well as to exchange ideas with your peers."

He paused for a moment, then continued, allowing his voice to harden noticeably.

"As such, you are expected to conduct yourselves as mature, responsible adults, not as bickering children. Our agenda will require at least four days to cover, but it will take four months if you cannot contain yourselves. Now, if you will resume your seats, I would like to continue with the subject at hand."

The group began to obediently sort themselves out and shuffle toward their seats. One captain, however, remained in place. She was short, middle-aged, and grossly overweight, but her ferocious expression gave her additional stature as she waved her hand in the air, demanding recognition.

"Yes, Momma?" Tambu asked, acknowledging the woman's hand.

"I think what you said points out our need to limit the size of the fleet " she declared without preamble. "We're getting too big to function effectively, even in a meeting like this."

"Am I to understand that you feel being too big has hampered your effectiveness?" Tambu quipped, deliberately misunderstanding in an effort to lighten the mood.

The group chuckled appreciatively, but Momma was not to be sidetracked.

"Not me, the fleet," she insisted.

"Plans for expansion are on the agenda for tomorrow," Tambu pointed out. "I would appreciate it if you would hold your comments and opinions until that time."

"Well, I want to put a motion on the agenda then," Momma pressed stubbornly. "I think we should put a top limit of a hundred ships on the fleet."

Tambu noted the murmurs and nods of assent among the other captains. There were also several angry faces and hands being thrust violently into the air. The meeting was poised on the brink of another argumentative digression if he didn't exert control immediately.

"Momma," he asked, "are you volunteering to withdraw your membership from the fleet?"

"Me?" the woman blinked, taken aback. "No! I never said that."

"The fleet is already over a hundred strong," Tambu pointed out solemnly. "To adopt or even consider your proposal would imply a willingness to remove several existing member ships from the roster. I assume you would not suggest such a thing unless you were ready to accept the same exile as you were suggesting for others."

"No," Momma admitted, "I—I didn't know there were that many ships already."

Defeated, she sank into a chair, avoiding the eyes of

the other captains. Tambu deliberately waited several
moments before offering a lifeline.

"You have raised a good point, one I feel all the captains should ponder prior to our expansion discussion
tomorrow. The subject currently under consideration,
though, is the treatment of our crewmen during their
visits planetside."

Several hands went up, seeking recognition. Tambu's
attention, however, was drawn to one figure whose
raised hand was accompanied by a thoughtful expression, a marked contrast to the eager or angry faces
around him.

"Yes, Puck?" Tambu asked.

"I've been listening for the past hour, and it seems to
me we're saying the same thing over and over. Now, we
could all take turns telling horror stories and have a lot
of fun one-upping each other and get everyone all
worked up, but I don't see much point in it. We're all in
agreement that our crews are being treated shabbily.
Once that's been established, I think it's a waste of time
to continue recounting the gory details. The real question we should be discussing is what are we going to do
about it?"

There was scattered applause as Puck sat down.
Tambu smiled to himself. Puck had come a long way
from the cocky, hair-trigger kid he used to be. He was
rapidly becoming one of the most valuable and popular
captains in the fleet.

"I think Puck has put his finger on the problem,"
Tambu announced firmly. "If we can dispense with
further itemizing of complaints, I'd like to hear some
discussion from the floor as to proposed courses of
action."

"We've got to hit them back," Blackjack called, leap-
ing to his feet. "As long as the Groundhogs think they
can gang up on our crewmembers and get away with it,
they're going to keep doing it. I say we should teach

them that if they lean on someone off a Tambu ship, they're going to get it shoved back down their throats."

Tambu frowned at the growls of assent that responded to Blackjack's suggestion.

"Whitey?" he said, recognizing the scowl on her face.

"We can't do that, Blackjack," she argued. "Last time I checked, we were still a law enforcement organization. Now, the one rule that's always held for law enforcement groups is that to gain and keep public support, you can't use undue force. That means if someone jostles you on the street, you can't break his arm. If we start going around exacting vengeance with interest for every insult or injury, we'll never get any public support."

"Public support?" Blackjack roared. "The last public support my ship got put three of my crew in the hospital!"

"How do you know your roughnecks didn't start it?" Whitey challenged.

"Three men don't start a fight with a whole bar," Blackjack shot back.

"They might," Whitey corrected. "Or they might try to hassle a hooker with a lot of friends."

"Are you saying my men—"

"That's enough!" Tambu barked. "It was decided that we weren't going to discuss specific incidents, nor am I going to allow this discussion to degenerate into childish name-calling."

Though they couldn't see him, the anger in his voice was sufficient to subdue the two combatants.

"Now then, Blackjack, you've proposed a program of retribution. Whitey has raised two questions. First, how much force are you suggesting we employ; and second, what level of investigation do you plan to carry out before launching your retribution? I am also curious as to your answers to those questions. Would you care to comment?"

"I haven't thought it through that far," Blackjack ad-

mitted. "I was just suggesting it as a possible solution
for discussion."

"I see," Tambu commented. "Very well, does anyone else have anything they'd like to add to this
proposal?"

Cowboy, the lanky captain of the *Whiplash*, rose
slowly to his feet.

"Ah'd like to add a thing er two to what Whitey said.
My paw, he used to be a policeman, and I learned a lot
listenin' to him talk over dinner."

"Is that how you managed to dodge the law for so
long?" someone quipped from the back of the room.

Cowboy shrugged and smiled, drawing a round of
laughter from the assemblage.

"Anyway," he continued, "Paw used to say anytime
there was a fight, both sides would insist the other side
started it. Usually they weren't even tryin' to cover up or
anythin'; they really believed it was the other folks
doin'. More often 'n not, my paw never could sort out
whose fault it really was."

He paused to look around the room.

"Now Ah'm not sayin' it's always our fault when
there's a fight, but Ah don't think we kin always say it's
the Groundhogs' fault neither. What's more, Ah don't
think that even if we tried to investigate each problem
that anyone'd believe we was bein' fair and impartial.
Heck, Ah don't think we'd believe it ourselves."

"But we can't just ignore it!" Blackjack roared, surg-
ing to his feet again. "Just because I don't have a plan
doesn't mean we should just sit back and do nothing.
Our crews are being discriminated against. We owe it to
them to take some kind of firm action."

Several voices rose in both support and protest, but
Tambu cut the growing pandemonium short.

"Jelly," he said, "I believe you're next as soon as we
have some quiet."

"Thank you, sir." The old man bowed as the voices
died down around him. "I would contest Mr.

Blackjack's last comment. I do not feel our crews are being singled out for special treatment."

There were several growls at this; but for the most part, the audience held its peace, waiting for the old captain to have his say.

"Mr. Cowboy's father was a policeman. Well, I was a policeman, too. Incidents such as those which have been recounted here, beatings, attempted rapes, minor extortion by spaceport personnel, are not unique to members of our fleet. Police blotters are filled to overflowing with such cases, and have been since long before our fleet was established. The areas we most often frequent planetside—the bars, the places of amusement which surround the spaceports—have always experienced a higher than average occurrence of such crimes. I feel we are reacting emotionally because our friends and families are directly involved. I am concerned, as all of you are, but I cannot believe we are victims of a vast conspiracy on the part of the planets, or that the authorities sanction such activities against us."

"What about the times when the police have been directly involved with the beatings?" someone called angrily.

"Unscrupulous men in law enforcement uniforms are neither new nor rare," Jelly argued. "It is sad, but a part of reality. I still feel it is the work of individuals rather than of some sanctioned group."

"That's real pretty, Jelly," Ramona challenged, "but I don't buy it. My crew and I have been cruising the starlanes for a long time and had our share of hassles with the Groundhogs, but nothing like we've been getting lately. You can't convince me that what's been happening is just random street violence."

Tambu raised his eyebrows. Until now he hadn't been aware of how deep Ramona's feelings ran on this subject.

Individual arguments were raging among the captains again as he cleared his throat to restore order. This time, however, someone beat him to it.

"Shut up! All of you!"

The naked rage in the voice cut through the clamor like a sword stroke, and the captains abruptly lapsed into silence and gave ground from its point of origin. Exposed by the crowd's parting was a pixie-ish woman, standing tall on a chair. Her skin was poisonously mottled, marking her as a victim of New Leprosy. Though hers was an arrested case, many still felt uneasy in her presence.

"The chair recognizes A.C.," Tambu smiled.

The irony of his voice was lost on the stormy woman as she launched into her tirade.

"Never in my entire life have I heard such crybaby moaning and weeping," she announced bluntly. "Screw what Cowboy and Jelly are saying. I'll give you what you want to hear: 'We're being picked on . . . discriminated against.' So what!"

The assembled captains sat in stunned silence as she continued.

"Most of you don't know what discrimination is," A.C. challenged. "Well, I do. For eleven years now I've been a New Leper. No matter what laws have been passed, that's still a stigma I have to live with. Jelly there's a black. He's been discriminated against so long he doesn't even notice it anymore. A lot of you are other things that some people don't like: Orientals, Jews, witches, women, young, old, smart, dumb. You don't get hassled working for Tambu and instead of being grateful, you get spoiled rotten. You forget how unfair reality is!"

She dropped her eyes and took a deep breath as if trying to calm herself.

"You're discriminated against because you're different," she said softly. "You all are—your crews are. You ride around on ships instead of working in a hardware store down the street. You're transients on any planet, outside the local order. That makes you different. That's all it takes to have people envy, fear, and hate you all at once. You can't change that by breaking heads, just like you can't change that by acting nice and polite. You don't change it at all. You learn to live with it."

A.C.'s head came up and her voice hardened.

"There are only two options to that. You can be stampeded into damnfool useless action, letting any ignorant spaceport bum who mouths off or takes a swing at you control your actions, or you can tuck your tails between your legs and quit. I don't know about the rest of you, but it'll take a lot worse than what I've heard today before I holler for help or quit. If any of you or your crews can't take a few lumps in stride, I say good-bye and good riddance. Go ahead and fold, but don't try to justify your own weakness by asking the whole fleet to follow suit."

There was total silence when A.C. sat down. Tambu waited several moments, then cleared his throat.

"I think I've heard enough discussion to reach a decision," he announced. "Until further notice, my orders on the matter are this: any incidents or complaints concerning fleet members and planetside citizenry are to be reviewed as individual isolated affairs and will be resolved in cooperation with planetside officials. While fleet members are allowed and expected to defend themselves if attacked, no retaliation in excess of the affront will be tolerated. Should there be any doubt as to the proper course of action in such an incident, or if a question arises as to interpretation of these orders, a priority call will be made to me so that I can personally guide the decision."

Tambu paused for a moment as he always did before concluding a ruling.

"Any captain who feels he cannot obey this order or enforce it within his crew rosters should signify it at this time. If a majority of captains so object, I will either reconsider my order or step down as fleet commander. If those objecting are in the minority, they will be removed from the rosters of the fleet. Those who do not object are thereby accepting the order and will be subject to discipline if it is breached. Dissenters, show yourselves at this time by standing.''

There was a shifting of chairs as the captains craned their necks to look around the room, but no one stood.

"Very well. As the hour is late, I adjourn the meeting for today. I believe the *Raven*'s crew has prepared refreshments for you, but remember, we reconvene tomorrow at 0800 hours, shiptime."

With that, he clicked off his console and sagged back in his chair. Though a decanter of wine was just a few steps away, he was too weary to fetch it. All energy seemed to drain out of him as soon as he adjourned the meeting.

He was suddenly aware that his shirt was drenched with sweat, and shook his head in dull recognition of the emotional output necessary to control these meetings. The fleet was a tiger—a multi-headed, multi-personalitied tiger. It would turn on the planets, on itself, or on him if he relaxed his control, however briefly. Like a wild-animal trainer, he only had his belief in his own goals and abilities to buoy him, and that only gave him limited control. If he tried to clamp down too hard, all hell would break loose.

Leaning back, he began to mentally review the arguments surrounding the fleet's planetside difficulties. He always did this after a major decision, probing for prejudices or hasty thought on his part, as well as any lingering resistance or resentment among the captains. Later, he would review the actual recordings of the meeting, but for the first pass he relied on his memory and impressions.

Cowboy's oration had been disappointing. His argument had supported Tambu's position of inaction, but in this case that support was annoying. From numerous arguments in the months prior to the meeting, Tambu knew that Cowboy personally favored retaliation, yet today he had spoken in favor of moderation.

A generous interpretation of the lanky captain's change of heart would be that his opinions had been over ruled by his crew, and that he was speaking today as their representative. A more probable explanation supported criticism voiced by both Ramona and Whitey as to the value of the yearly meetings.

They steadfastly maintained that most of the captains—particularly the newer ones—were not voicing their true feelings in the discussions, but rather attempting to curry favor with Tambu by saying what they thought he wanted to hear. While Tambu argued firmly that this was not the case, he had to admit to himself that he had no way of knowing for sure—and hearing Cowboy contradict himself made him wonder anew if he was deluding himself as to the sincerity of the captains' statements.

An insistent chiming interrupted his thoughts, and he looked to his console. The priority call light flashed red, drawing a frown to his face.

There was supposed to be a ban on personal conferences for the duration of the meetings, sparing him the annoyance of captains "stumping" for support of their proposals. For a moment he considered ignoring the call, then he noticed it was coming from the Raven. Was there trouble among the captains? A duel?

With a sigh, he activated the viewscreen once more. To his surprise, however, it was Egor's face, not Whitey's that appeared on the display.

"What's wrong, Egor?" Tambu asked, instantly regretting having spoken. If he had kept quiet, Egor never would have known that his call was answered.

"Nothing's wrong," Egor answered hastily. "Whitey let me use her gear to call you is all."

"There are to be no personal conferences until the

meetings are over," Tambu growled. "If there is no emergency, then—"

"It's not an emergency, but it's important," Egor interrupted. "I thought you'd want to talk it over with me first, but if you're too busy, we'll do it from the floor during the meeting."

There was a warning tone in the big man's voice that caught Tambu's attention. Swallowing his annoyance, he leaned into the mike again to apologize.

"Sorry to be so abrupt, my friend, but these meetings always set me on edge. That's part of why I avoid personal conferences until they're over—it keeps me from taking my frustrations out on people close to me. What was it you wished to discuss?"

The anger drained from Egor's face, and he dropped his eyes.

"I would like—I want you to relieve me of command," he said softly.

Tambu's annoyance flared anew, but he kept it out of his voice.

"Why?" he asked.

"These yearly meetings emphasize something we've both known for a long time now. I'm no leader. I don't belong in the same room with these others."

"You're a captain, the same as they are," Tambu retorted. "I fail to see the difference."

"The other captains know their crews," Egor protested. "When they talk at the meetings they speak as representatives of their ships."

"And you?" Tambu pressed.

"My crew doesn't like me. I don't know their minds or how they feel on the issues. I can run a ship, but I'm clumsy with people. Please. I'm asking as an old friend. Put someone else in my place. Let me go back to crewing like I did before."

"What makes you think the other captains know what their crews want?"

"It's obvious. You can see it in their stance and hear it in their voices when they talk."

"They don't know their crews any better than you do," Tambu declared harshly. "You're confusing good oratory with good leadership."

Egor frowned, trying to grasp the concept as Tambu continued.

"Look, Egor, a lot of those captains aren't as sensitive as you are. It never occurs to them that their crew might have opinions. They speak their own minds and assume their crews are in agreement with them. A lot more know their crews don't agree with them, but they don't care. They're the captains, and that's that."

"Are you sure?" Egor asked suspiciously.

"In my position, I can see it. If I were going to single out poor leaders for replacement, it would be those captains, not you. Most of them are Johnny-come-latelies who substitute words for action. Their records are so empty that they have to save their arms to call attention to each little victory. You've successfully commanded a ship for me for nearly five years now, Egor. Your record speaks for itself."

"But my crew doesn't like me," Egor insisted with characteristic doggedness.

"I'm running a business, not a popularity contest!" Tambu exploded. "Can't you get that through your head? Your crew is working because they're getting paid, not because they have any great love for you—or me, for that matter. As long as they're doing their jobs, then you're doing yours. Beyond that I don't want to hear about it."

The words hung heavy in the air as Egor stared out of the viewscreen at him with a frozen expression.

"You're right," the big man said at last, not changing his expression. "I shouldn't have bothered you."

"Egor," Tambu began, his anger gone, "my friend, I—"

"Don't worry," Egor interrupted levelly, "I'll command my ship for you. I'll command it for you until you remove me yourself. Egor out."

The viewscreen went blank.

Tambu sat motionless, staring at the screen and trying to remember when, if ever, a captain had broken with him instead of vice versa.

INTERVIEW VII

"It sounds as if those yearly meetings were quite something," Erickson commented.

"They still are," Tambu said. "The captains' meetings are still one of the high points on the fleet's yearly calendar. Though they are usually much calmer than the episode I just mentioned, occasionally they can become as spirited and emotional as those conducted during our formative years."

"Yet despite their emotional outbursts, they seem to be fairly levelheaded when it comes to advice or debate."

"Never underestimate the abilities of a ship captain," Tambu warned. "No matter how often I tell myself that, I still forget sometimes that just because someone dresses funny or doesn't speak well doesn't mean he is any less capable or intelligent. To survive as a ship captain, particularly a fighting ship captain, requires a wide range of skills and abilities. One must be a tactician, a diplomat, a father-confessor, a personnel manager, and an accountant all rolled into one. Then, on top of it all, be a leader: one who can command and get respect and cooperation from a wide range of individuals."

"I must admit that's a different array of characteristics than has been displayed when one of your captains has been interviewed by the press," Erickson observed, cautiously.

"Of course it is!" Tambu snapped. "When you interview someone, they'll tell you what they think you want to hear. Not that they'll lie to you, mind you—just change their priorities and emphasis a bit."

"Then the captains have been deliberately trying to create the impressions they have?" the reporter blinked.

"Certainly. First of all, a captain is an administrator. If a captain tried to tell you about drudgery and paperwork involved in his job, you'd lose interest. Instead, they tell you all about the dangers of space, the ship-to-ship duels, and the harrowing escapes they've had— much of which is simply rehashings of stories they've read in adventure novels."

"And of course reporters like me eat it up," Erickson smiled appreciatively. "Tell me, do you think this editing of information is unique to ship captains?"

"Not at all. I feel it's a normal human tendency. If I asked you to tell me what it was like being a reporter, would you tell me about having to write stories about things that didn't interest you, while older, less capable reporters got the prime assignments? Or would you regale me with tales about gathering news under dangerous conditions and bravely exposing the truth despite the pressures of a corrupt establishment?"

"Touché! It sounds like you know the news business."

"I know people," Tambu corrected. "I have to. In your line of work, if you make an error in judging people, you lose a story. If I make an error, people die. It's a great incentive for me to get to know people as well as is humanly possible."

"Yet you still make mistakes," Erickson noted quickly.

"Too often," Tambu admitted. "But then, at the stakes I'm playing at, one mistake every five years is too often."

"I can see why you established the yearly captain's meetings. That's a lot of weight for anybody to carry alone. At least the meetings let you spread the responsibility around a little."

"Yes and no. While the discussions are helpful, the final decisions are still mine. I've discovered that having additional viewpoints and opinions does not always ease the decision-making process. Then, too, I have to make independent decisions on things which arise between meetings."

"Could you estimate a percentage split as to the number of decisions that come out of the meetings versus those that are made unilaterally?"

"No, I couldn't. There have been so many decisions made over the course of my career that I literally couldn't count them, much less divide them into categories. What's more, the varying magnitude of the problems would make a numerical comparison meaningless."

"I see. Well, how about decisions of major importance or impact? Would you have a feel for that?"

"I'm afraid the answer is still no," Tambu replied, but more hesitantly. "I've never thought of decisions in numerical terms. If I correctly interpret the direction of your questioning, however, there was one specific major decision I recall having to make unilaterally. I also recall that it was one of the most difficult decisions I've ever had to make."

CHAPTER SEVEN

Tambu sat alone, slouched at his command console. The viewscreen display showed the starfields outside, but his eyes were directed at the cabin wall, unfocused and unfeeling.

Moving as if it were not a part of him, his hand picked up the decanter to fill the wineglass before him. Only after setting the vessel down and raising the glass to his lips did he realize that both glass and decanter were empty.

Annoyance and puzzlement filled his mind as he frowned at the glass, momentarily driving out all other thoughts.

How much had he drunk? He wanted another glass, but knew he had to keep his mind clear to sort out the current situation. Had he filled the decanter this morning? How long ago was morning?

He ran a weary hand over his chin and noted with some surprise the well-developed stubble which met his touch. It had obviously been more than twelve hours since he shaved, but he couldn't remember shaving.

With a growl of self-disgust, he pushed the glass and decanter away from him. If he couldn't even remember what time of day it was, he certainly was in no condition to drink.

"Are you with us again?"

Tambu turned his head slowly and found Ramona perched on the foot of his bed. He hadn't heard her come in and didn't have the faintest idea how long she had been there.

"I'm sorry, love," he apologized, smiling faintly as he stretched. "My mind must have drifted a bit. Did you say something?"

Ramona shook her head.

"You know, lover, for a grim, humorless type, at times you have an incredible talent for understatement."

"Meaning what?"

"Meaning this is the first time you've come up for air in over two days. When your mind drifts, you don't kid around!"

"Two days!" Tambu exclaimed, ignoring her jibe. "What happened? Was I drinking? What about the fleet?"

"Whoa!" Ramona interrupted, holding up her hand. "The fleet's fine—or as good as could be expected. You haven't been drinking, you've been working. Nonstop. What's more, you worked thirty hours straight before you stopped talking to me or acknowledging there was anything in the universe except you and that damned viewscreen."

"But the fleet's all right?" Tambu pressed. "Who's been handling their calls?"

"You have. But I'll bet you couldn't tell me who you talked with or what they said without looking at your notes."

"You're right," he admitted ruefully. "I can remember generalities, but not specifics. I guess I'd better review this mess before I go any farther."

"Not so fast! The other side of the coin is that you haven't eaten or slept in that whole time. Now that you're back in the land of the living, I'm not going to let you plunge into this again until you take care of yourself."

"But I've got to reach a decision on this—and soon! I've already stalled too long. The fleet's counting on me."

"Sure, the fleet's counting on you," Ramona argued. "So what happens to the fleet if you end up in sick bay from exhaustion and malnutrition? I'll give you two choices: Either make your decision now, if you won't rest until it's done; or if you want more time to ponder the problem, rest, then make your decision. One of the two, but I want you in bed in the next fifteen minutes!"

Normally, Tambu would have been livid if any of his captains—even Ramona—had tried to give him orders. But now, he couldn't even muster the interest or energy to argue. This, more than anything else, indicated to him that she was probably right.

"All right," he sighed, shooting a covert glance at the console's call board. "But wake me up again in a couple of hours."

"I'll try once after six hours. But if you won't budge, I'll let you get another four."

"Under no circumstances more than eight," he insisted. "Even if you have to throw ice water on me. I've got to get this problem resolved."

"Agreed," Ramona nodded, rising to her feet. "I'll run down to the galley and swipe a couple of sandwiches for you. If you doze off, they'll be here on the side table when you wake up—and quit looking at the call board! I'm giving orders to put any incoming calls on hold until you wake up."

"Not the blinkers!" Tambu ordered, his head coming up with a snap. "I'm not going to lose a ship because I need a little sleep!"

Ramona chewed her lip.

"Can I try to do a little screening?" she asked hesitantly. "We both know that some of the captains abuse the emergency priority to get your attention."

"Very well," Tambu agreed wearily. "But I want to take any genuine emergencies."

"I know." Ramona stooped to give him a quick kiss. "That's why you're top dog in this outfit."

He remained seated at the console for several minutes after her departure, pondering the true nature of his current status. Was he top dog? He didn't feel like it. There was no power or joy in his routine—only incredible fear.

It was as if he was at the controls of a ground skimmer with the throttle jammed wide open, trying desperately to avoid obstacles darting at him from the distance, fighting certain knowledge that eventually he would react too slowly or steer in the wrong direction. The longer he survived, the faster the skimmer was going, making the inevitable crash that much more terrible when it finally came.

With effort, he closed his mind against the image. Ramona was right. He needed sleep, if only to steel his nerves.

He was stretching his legs, preparing to rise from his seat, when a chime sounded and a light came on the console.

Tambu smiled as he looked at the signal. Ramona was slipping. The light was red, but not blinking. Either she hadn't issued her orders yet, or a call managed to slip past her blockade.

His eye fell on the indicator, and his smile faded abruptly. The call was from the *Raven*! From Whitey! Whitey had never used a priority signal of any kind.

Without thinking, his hand went to the transmission switch.

"Tambu here," he said even before the signal appeared on his screen. "What's the problem, Whitey?"

Whitey's face appeared on the screen, her features frozen in a mask of anger.

"Tambu?" she asked. "I want to know what's going on!"

"About what?" Tambu blinked, then it all came back to him. Of course! That's what Whitey would be calling about.

"All right," Whitey snapped. "If you want to play games, we'll take it from the top. I was just down on Elei making our sales pitch. They were receptive—very receptive for a planet that had never agreed with our position before. They were so receptive, in fact, they wouldn't even let me talk. They just signed up—said they'd pay whatever we asked."

"And you want to know why," Tambu finished for her.

"I asked them why," Whitey spat. "And you know what they said? They said they were paying so my ship wouldn't burn their capital."

Tambu ran his fingers wearily through his hair, but didn't interrupt.

"Of course I laughed at that," Whitey continued bitterly. "I told them I was one of Tambu's captains and that Tambu doesn't operate that way. You know what they said to that?"

"They told you about what happened on Zarn," Tambu answered tonelessly.

For several moments Whitey stared at him out of the screen, her anger melting into hurt puzzlement.

"Then it's true?" she finally asked in a soft voice. "I was hoping they were lying—or had been lied to."

"It's true," Tambu admitted.

"And you want to know why I'm calling?" Whitey demanded, her anger returning in a rush. "What's going on in the fleet? We never agreed to anything like this."

"I doubt they told you the whole story," Tambu began.

"How many ways can you read the facts?" Whitey

interrupted. "One of our ships burns out a whole city—a city that has no way of fighting back. How can anybody justify that?"

"Nikki's dead," Tambu said softly.

"Nikki? Puck?" Whitey blinked. "What happened?"

"He went to pay a call on the Planetary Council, much as you did on Elei," Tambu explained. "It seems they not only refused our services, they were exceptionally unpleasant about it. Among other things, they stated that their planet was going to bar their spaceport to any of our ships."

"But spaceports are open to any ship, regardless of origin!" Whitey protested.

"That's right," Tambu confirmed. "But the Council seemed ready to overlook that detail, along with numerous other niceties humans usually extend to each other—niceties that usually transend planetary or racial differences. Anyway, to keep a long story short, Puck lost his temper and told him what he thought of them and their decisions. He was complete enough in his oration that he finished it by spitting on the floor, whereupon the Council guards shot him down in cold blood."

"Good God!" Whitey gasped. "What did they do to the guards?"

"Nothing," Tambu replied grimly. "Not only were the guards not disciplined, the Council had his body delivered back to the ship's shuttlecraft with the message that he was to be taken off-planet for burial. I believe the specific quote was they 'didn't want him or scum like him on their planet, alive or dead.' Shortly thereafter, his ship opened fire on the capital."

"You're sure he didn't attack them physically?" Whitey pressed.

"He was alone and unarmed, Whitey," Tambu said softly. "When they carried his body through the streets to the spaceport, the crowds cheered the guards and spit on his body."

"How do you know all this if he was alone?" Whitey challenged.

"From reports submitted by our informants who were there at the time. I've even got copies of the official reports of the incident prepared by the Council guardsmen. Most of my time since the blow-up has been spent piecing the facts together and checking them."

"You mean you ordered the strike *before* you checked the story?" Whitey exploded.

"I didn't order it at all, Whitey. I didn't even approve it."

"You didn't?" Whitey's face showed a mixture of relief and concern. "Then who did?"

"Puck's second in command—with the full support of the crew." Tambu sighed. "Puck was a very popular captain."

Whitey rubbed her forehead absently as if trying to erase her frown wrinkles.

"I still don't think they were justified, hitting the whole city that way," she said at last.

"They didn't mean to hit the whole city," Tambu said quietly. "They were trying for the Council Building. It might have worked, except for two things. Nobody has any experience shooting at a planetside target from space. They missed—missed badly. They also under-estimated the devastation caused by weapons designed for long-range work in space."

They both lapsed into silence again, each lost in their own thoughts.

"I wish you had told me sooner," Whitey commented finally. "It was bad, hearing it the way I did. I don't know which was worse; the news itself or hearing from someone outside the fleet."

"I'm sorry," Tambu said sincerely. "I've been trying to put together a new policy statement for general release, and it isn't easy. I've been trying to alert any captain due for planetfall, but the *Raven* wasn't due at

Elei for another two days."

"Puck was a friend of mine," Whitey observed dryly. "You might have made an exception to your rules in this case."

"I said I was busy!" Tambu snarled. "What do you think I do with my time? Sit on my butt and play darts? I would have called you if I could, but I couldn't. There were more important things to do. I don't like saying that, but that's the way it is. The good of the fleet has to take precedence over my personal friendships."

"What's so all-fired important?" Whitey challenged. "How long does it take you to issue a statement saying you had nothing to do with Zarn—that the ship was acting against your orders and is going to be disciplined?"

"It—it isn't as simple as that," Tambu replied hesitant for the first time in the conversation. "There are a lot of factors to be considered."

"Like what?" Whitey pressed. "Don't you realize that the longer you let things sit without comment, the more people are going to assume you ordered the strike?"

"I realize it . . . more than you do, Whitey. As far as our personal friendship goes, I should tell you that except for the crew of Puck's ship and myself, you're the only one who knows I didn't order the strike."

"You mean you're going to take the blame for Zarn?" Whitey gaped. "Why, Tambu? You weren't responsible."

"They're a ship under my command," Tambu countered. "Technically, that makes me responsible. I've taken a lot of indirect credit in the past for things my captains did. I can't just wash my hands of what happened because things went sour."

"I don't agree. But even if I did . . . if I felt you were responsible, it doesn't change anything. You've got to do something. You've got to level some kind of punishment against the ship."

"For what?" Tambu demanded. "For being loyal to their captain? For going after a bunch of bastards who think they have the right to gun down anyone from one of my ships?"

"How about for leveling a city and everybody in it?" Whitey shot back. "Don't you think that was a little extreme?"

"Yes, I do," Tambu retorted. "But I'm in a bad position to judge. I haven't set foot off a ship in over six years. I don't know how bad things are for the crews when they go planetside. I've got no comprehension of what they've been putting up with. You tell me, Whitey. If things had worked out differently—if you had been gunned down on Elei instead of Puck getting killed on Zarn, how would your crew react?"

"I—I don't know," Whitey admitted. "I'd like to think they'd react with more restraint."

"But you can't be sure," Tambu pointed out viciously. "Okay, let's go a step further. If they reacted the same way Puck's crew did . . . if they did that and you were in my position, what would you do to them? What kind of punishment would you level? A wrist-slap? Would you have them all hunted down and executed? What?"

"I'd have to think about it. I can't just come up with an answer on something that big."

"Then why are you leaning on me for trying to take time to think?" Tambu accused. "Do you think I've been planning in advance for this? Am I supposed to have a master plan in mind for every disaster?"

"Okay! I was out of line! But you've had time now. You'd better come up with something fast. Lord knows how the planets will react when they hear—or the rest of the fleet, for that matter."

Fatigue made Tambu's laugh harsh.

"Do you want to know how they're reacting? Over two-thirds of the fleet has called in already. Less than three percent have objected to what happened—and the main protest there was they they weren't notified in advance of the policy change. That's how upset the fleet is!"

"But the planets—"

"Right along with those call-ins," Tambu inter-rupted, "came a tidal wave of sign-ons. Our crews don't even have to go planetside and ask anymore. Planets are calling them to subscribe. Some of them are relaying calls through other planets. Financially, this is the best thing that's ever happened to the fleet. We could cut our fees by a third tomorrow and still show a profit."

He suddenly noticed that Whitey was shrinking on the viewscreen. Not that the reception was bad, but rather that she seemed to be sagging . . . folding in on herself.

"Are you all right?" he asked, suddenly solicitous. "I didn't mean to shout at you. It's just that things have been pretty rough at this end."

Whitey shook her head, but this time she didn't raise her eyes.

"That's all right. It's what you're saying, not how you're saying it that's made up my mind."

"Made up your mind about what?" Tambu frowned.

"I'm quitting," Whitey sighed. "Getting out while the getting's good. I'll recommend Pepe, my second-in-command, as my replacement. He's as solid as they come, and the crew respects him."

"Wait a minute," Tambu protested. "I haven't reached a decision on this mess yet. Don't—"

"Yes, you have,' Whitey corrected gently. "You may not know it yet, but you have. I know you, Tambu. Maybe better than you know yourself. If you were going to jump the way I think you should, you would have done it by now. Just the fact that you're still seesawing back and forth tells me something. It tells me I can't follow you any more."

Tambu felt the truth in her words wash over him as

she spoke, though he wouldn't admit it even to himself.

"Isn't this a bit sudden?" he asked quietly.

"Not really. I've thought about doing it a hundred times since we started. I want out, but it has to be sudden. I can't ease away from it."

Unlike his conversations with Egor, Tambu knew instinctively that he could not argue or wheedle Whitey into changing her mind once it was made up.

"Very well. It will take some time to make the arrangements. You're due a substantial pension—and we'll have to set up a cover for you."

"Put my pension in the general fund. I've saved enough on my own to live on. As for a cover, I figure I'll just have the shuttle run me down to Elei and settle there. It's as good a place as any."

"But on Elei they know you're one of my captains," Tambu objected. "It shouldn't be safe."

"They'll also know I've quit the fleet," Whitey pointed out. "And why. I don't think I'll have much trouble."

"It sounds like you've thought this through pretty carefully," Tambu observed bitterly.

"I've given it some thought, ever since they gave me the news on Elei. Just for the record, Tambu, I think you're wrong. The fleet was never popular with the planets before, but now you're taking on the role of an extortionist. I don't think they'll put up with that for long. There's going to be trouble, and I for one don't want to be around when it hits."

"That's one person's opinion."

"Maybe," Whitey shrugged. "But then again, maybe it's the opinion of a whole lot of people. You should listen to the folks planetside as much as you do to the people in your fleet."

"At the moment, I'm more concerned with my fleet."

"I know," Whitey sighed. "That's were you're going wrong. Good-bye, Tambu. Whitey out."

Ramona reentered the cabin in time to see the view-screen fading to darkness.

"What was all that about?" she asked. "I thought you weren't going to take any more calls until after you got some sleep."

"That was a call from the *Raven*," Tambu explained, staring at the dark screen. "We just lost another captain—the hard way."

"Whitey?" Ramona exclaimed, setting down the tray she was carrying and moving to his side, "Whitey's been killed?"

Tambu rose and started for the bed, ignoring the sandwiches on the tray.

"No, she wasn't killed. But we still lost her the hard way."

INTERVIEW VIII

Erickson was silent for several minutes after Tambu finished his narrative.

"So that's the way it actually happened," he said at last.

"Yes," Tambu sighed. "That's how it happened. You may use it in your article, if you wish. Enough incidents have occurred since then, it is now an item of historic curiosity more than anything else. I don't believe it will change anyone's mind one way or the other."

"It's certainly given me something to think about."

"But it hasn't changed your mind noticeably. You disapproved of the Zarn incident before, and you still do . . . regardless of the circumstances."

"You're right," Erickson admitted. "But I will say I'm glad the decision wasn't mine to make."

"In case you ponder the problem at leisure sometime in the future, let me give you one extra thought to complicate things. I believe that we are in agreement that if consulted in advance, neither of us would have ordered the strike on Zarn. Remember, though, that you're trying to put yorself in my place, and that means deciding a course of action after the fact. By the time I entered the picture, the strike was already over—and nothing I could do or say would change that."

"So the real question was whether to atone for the deed or capitalize on it."

"That's right," Tambu acknowledged. "I chose to capitalize on it. Even in hindsight, I don't know how we could have atoned for what happened. Perhaps it was weak of me, but it was easier to take advantage of the situation."

"But was it an advantage?" Erickson pressed. "I mean, it seems to me in the long run it would have been better business if you could have disassociated yourself and the fleet from the incident."

"I fear you're a better reporter than a businessman, Mr. Erickson. There were many factors I took into consideration in that decision, most of which were business oriented. Group image: I don't feel it would have enhanced our position to let it be known to the planets that they could kill our crew members and throw us off-planet without repercussions. Internal morale: It would have had an adverse effect on our crewmen if they were to feel the hierarchy of the fleet not only did not act when one of ours was attacked, but punished them when they performed what in their eyes was a demonstration of loyalty and affection. Profit and loss: I've already pointed out that our list of subscribers increased substantially after the incident. As far as business goes, my decision was actually quite wise."

"But isn't part of business catering to one's public image? You could have avoided a lot of bad feeling if the criminal label had not been attached to you and your fleet."

"Could we?" Tambu asked sarcastically. "If you recall, even before the incident at Zarn, we were being treated like criminals or worse. If given a choice between being viewed with contempt or with fear, we'll take fear. Zarn gave us that choice."

"So, in your opinion, Zarn actually made things easier for the fleet," Erickson suggested, eager to move the interview away from the delicate subject.

"I did not mean to imply that. Richer does not equate with easier. In many ways, our newfound success increased our internal problems. In fact, there were so many decisions to be made that really important issues tended to be lost in the shuffle. Some decisions I made in haste—assuming them to be minor—came back later to haunt me mercilessly."

CHAPTER EIGHT

"Coffee, love?" Ramona asked, poking her head into Tambu's cabin.

"Thanks, I could use a break."

"We finally found our problem." Ramona gave him a steaming cup and curled up in a nearby chair. "It took three rounds of check-inspections, but we found it."

"Where was it?" Tambu asked curiously.

"There was a flaw in one of the circuit boards in the Emergency Life Support Override System. It took only three minutes to replace—once we found it. Could have been nasty if we hadn't caught it, though."

Tambu frowned.

"Isn't that a sealed system? When was it last inspected?"

"Two years ago," Ramona recited. "During its scheduled preventative maintenance cycle."

"Then the problem's been with us that long?" Tambu winced.

"No," Ramona insisted firmly. "It's a recent development."

"You seem awfully sure of that."

"I am, for two reasons. First, it was triple-checked during that inspection. I know the crewmembers whose initials were on the seal. They aren't the kind who would fake an inspection or miss a defect that obvious."

"And the other reason?"

"The other reason is the tapping started only recently."

"I thought so." Tambu smiled. "You know, sometimes I wonder if superstitions would survive if we didn't force feed them."

"Now, look," Ramona flared, "I'm not saying I believe in all the superstitions that we keep in space, but the tapping on the outer hull of a ship as a warning of impending disaster is fairly well documented."

"By searching until something wrong is found?" Tambu teased. "In any network of circuits and machinery as complex as a ship, at any given point in time, a close inspection would reveal something wrong. Are you trying to say you honestly believe that if we had inspected that system, say, a week ago, that we wouldn't have found the flaw?"

Ramona glared. "All I know is that on five separate occasions I've been on board a ship when the tapping was heard. Each time a pending malfunction was found. That's enough to convince me to stop everything and run a check-inspection if we hear it again. Wouldn't you?"

"Sure I would," Tambu acknowledged. "But even though I keep the superstitions right along with everybody else, there's part of my mind that reminds me that what I'm doing is silly. You'd think man would have outgrown such childishness, but instead we find technology and superstition advancing hand in hand down the starlanes. I just find it a bit ironic is all."

"Well, I don't think we'll ever get away from it," Ramona grumbled, still annoyed at his teasing. "Let's

face it. Our crewmembers aren't the brightest representatives mankind can muster. A lot of them don't have
much education other than what they've picked up on
shipboard. That means they learn the superstitions right
along with everything else."

"Right," Tambu nodded. "Oh well, I'm glad we're
under way again. If that's the biggest hassle on this ship,
it's the shining star of the fleet."

"Speaking of shipboard hassles," Ramona said, "has
there been any more word about the crewman who died
on board the *Scorpion*?"

"As a matter of fact, the investigation's closed. The
final ruling is suicide."

"Suicide?" Ramona frowned. "Any report as to the
reason?"

"Space-depression." Tambu shrugged. "Egor says
the guy was a borderline basket case when he signed on.
Probably joined out of a death wish and decided to do it
himself when he found out how slow things really are
working for the fleet."

"Egor?" Ramona echoed. "You let Egor investigate it
himself?"

"I didn't *let* him do it," Tambu protested. "He did it
on his own initiative. Wouldn't you if it happened on
your ship?"

"Aren't you going to conduct your own investigation
as a check?"

"What for?" Tambu countered. "I have no reason to
doubt Egor's conclusions. I thought you were the one
who was always after me to delegate more and quit
trying to run everything personally."

"Maybe I shouldn't say this," Ramona hesitated,
pursing her lips, "but there have been a lot of rumors of
discontent on the *Scorpion*."

"You're right, you shouldn't say it," Tambu commented grimly. "There *are* problems on the *Scorpion*.
Egor has reported them to me himself, and the last thing

he needs right now are a lot of rumormongers fanning the flames."

"In that case, maybe I'd better take my rumors and leave."

"Hey, hey!" Tambu soothed, holding up a hand. "I'm sorry. I didn't mean to lean on you. Look, I know you're trying to help . . . and I appreciate it. It's just that I'm a bit on edge. I really hate wading through all this."

He gestured toward the table behind him.

"The yearly financial statements?" Ramona raised her eyebrows, her anger mollified by her curiosity. "I thought you *enjoyed* playing with numbers, love."

"There's a limit! Nine boxes of paper and data tapes is a bit much, even for me."

"Why don't you just review the summaries?" she suggested.

"These *are* the summaries. The support data behind them would fill several cargo holds."

"Well, it should solve your leisure-time problem," Ramona joked. "Seriously, though, why do you bother? I mean, just the fact that everyone has to submit yearly reports to you should serve as a deterrent against embezzlement without your having to review them all."

"Don't bet on it." Tambu sighed. "Sooner or later, people would figure it out if I just filed their reports. Sometimes . . . wait. Here, let me read this to you."

He fished around on the table for a specific sheet of paper, found it, held it aloft, and read:

"If you have gotten this far in our report, we will buy you a case of your favorite whiskey. Simply call so we know what brand to buy."

"Really?" Ramona laughed. "Are you going to collect?"

"I sure am," Tambu grinned. "And on the other eight notes like it I've found buried in other reports. I also get to send about a dozen terse reprimands to references to my parentage or sexual preferences."

"What are you going to do with all that liquor?" Ramona asked. "You don't drink anything but wine."

"Another year like this last one, and I'll be ready for the hard stuff. But, I can't actually accept the shipments. If nothing else, it would show which ship I was on. Instead, I'll have each donor send it off to a different ship, with a note that the ship's crew is to enjoy the gift with my compliments."

"Sounds like a good deal. Any chance my ship can get in on that?"

"I'll have to check my lists," he retorted with mock severity. "You know I won't play favorites. Just because you successfully seduced me doesn't mean you should expect special privileges."

"I stand duly chastised." She hung her head dramatically.

"Getting back to the original question, jokers like these would be able to tell in no time flat if I wasn't reading their reports."

"Which would be an open invitation to gimmick the books," Ramona acknowledged.

"Even if I trusted everyone implicitly, which I don't, but even if I did, I'd still take the time to review the reports. There's a lot of information here once you learn to read between the lines."

"Such as what?"

"Well," Tambu squinted, "I can tell how often they conduct target practice, what the condition of their ship is, the state of the crew's morale—"

"Wait a minute. You lost me. How can you tell all that from just looking at numbers?"

"By studying various expense items. For example, if a ship is spending less than half the amount on maintenance and parts as other ships the same size and age, I can make an educated guess that its condition is less than excellent."

"And crew morale?"

"If a captain is paying his crew low wages and is spending little or nothing on employee luxuries, they will be noticeably less happy than a well-paid crew on a ship with a new lounge and game room."

"I see," Ramona commented thoughtfully. "Maybe I should take another look at my own reports."

"I'm not sure how much good it would do you without other reports to compare it to. What you might do is call a couple of the other ships and ask for copies of their reports."

"I just might do that," Ramona nodded. "Now you've got me wondering."

Tambu's simply giving her copies of the reports submitted to him was not mentioned by either of them. Yearly reports were strictly confidential between Tambu and the individual captains.

Tambu continued, "Besides checking on individual ships, I use the reports to look for new ideas. There's one ship in the fleet, for example, that's shown significant savings on their food expenses by allowing planetside food services to open a franchise on board the ship. Food preparation and planning becomes the service's problem, and the crew buys their meals in a cafeteria."

"Interesting. Does it work?"

"I'm still checking into it," Tambu said. "Even though their food costs have been reduced, they've had to pay their crews more to cover the price of the meals. It could be a false savings."

"I can see where it gets a bit complicated," Ramona commented.

"Oh, that's not the complicated part," Tambu replied innocently. "Where it gets rough is trying to use the reports to find answers to nonspecific quantitative questions."

"You're showing off now!"

"You're right. But it's true nonetheless."

"I'll call your bluff," she challenged. "Give me an

example of a nonqualitative . . . whatever it was you said."

"Gladly. Do you remember the item on the agenda about next year's captains' meeting that calls for a review of the funds allocation methods?"

"I glanced over it, but I didn't read it carefully. Why?"

"You should look at it. It's going to be one of the hottest items on the agenda. Most of the other captains are gearing up for a major brawl."

"Maybe it's the terminology that's putting me off. What's it all about? In nonaccounting terms."

"Simply put, the planets who subscribe to our services pay their money into a big common pool," Tambu explained. "From that pool, the money gets divided down among the individual ships which comprise the fleet. The question that's being raised is what is a fair basis for determining which ship gets how much."

"Aside from the fact that everybody gets emotional when there's money on the line, what's the problem?" Ramona yawned. "I mean, how many ways can you carve a pie?"

"Lots. The trouble is, each way has its drawbacks."

He rose and began to pace the room as he spoke, unconsciously falling into a lecturer's role.

"We can't just give a set amount to each ship. Some of our ships are twice as big as others and require larger crews and more maintenance. Similarly, we can't give a set amount to each crewman or captain. On a small ship, a crewman has to do more than one job. Should a navigator gunner be paid the same as a man who is only a gunner?"

"Or should the captain of a five-man cruiser be paid as much as the captain of a forty-man dreadnought?" Ramona supplied.

"Exactly." Tambu nodded. "And then there's seniority. Should a five-year crewman be paid the same as someone in the same job who just signed on?"

"It *could* get a little sticky."

"I haven't even gotten to the good part yet. There's also the matter of the patrol range of the individual ship. If two ships are the same size with the same size crew, and one of them is patrolling eight planets and the other patrols twenty, should they be paid the same? Of course, there you have to figure in the currency exchange rates and price of supplies on the various planets."

"Stop!" Ramona cried. "Okay! I get the picture. It's a morass. What has all this got to do with the financial reports?"

"Between now and the meeting, I have to formulate a plan. If I don't have something firmly in mind before the item comes ups on the agenda, the discussion will degenerate into a dogfight."

He poked listlessly at the heap of paper and tapes on his table.

"Going through this stuff, I'm trying to find a pattern to our costs—by ship and by man. Then I get to sort through it again to define the modifying factors such as patrol sectors. Hopefully, then, I can rough out a proposal that will make everybody happy—or at least make everybody equally unhappy."

Ramona rose to her feet and stretched lazily.

"Well, this time I think I'm going to do what everybody else usually does."

"What's that?" Tambu asked.

"I'll let you figure it all out, argue for a while, then go along with what you propose. No sense in both of us losing sleep over this."

"But don't you want to conduct an investigation of your own to check against my findings?" Tambu gaped in mock horror.

She stuck her tongue out at him.

"Even if I had access to the data you've got, which I don't, I wouldn't know what to do with it—or have the time to do it if I did."

Tambu shook his head sharply as if trying to clear his ears.

"Could you repeat that last part? It didn't make any sense at all."

"Simply put," Ramona sniffed in imitation of his earlier lecture style, "I've got my hands full running my ship. Running the fleet's your job, and you're welcome to it! Bye now!"

Tambu laughed and returned her wave as she left. But after she was gone, his smile faded.

Even though she had been joking, she was right. The whole mess was sitting in his lap. It wasn't that the captains didn't care or that they weren't intelligent, it was just that no one else in the fleet had the overview he had when it came to problem solving. Ramona knew much more about the intricacies of running the fleet than she had shown during their conversation. It was obvious to Tambu that she had been playing 'straight man' to his show-off performance so that he would have a chance to talk things out a bit. Still, even she couldn't aid him directly in this work. Like the other captains, she lacked the detailed comparative data which currently only he had access to. The captains' jealous hoarding of information was inadvertently giving him sole propietorship of the job of fleet coordinator.

With a sigh, he started to turn towards the desk again when a light on his command console caught his eye. It was only an amber call—next to no importance or priority, but he was glad to answer it. Anything to stall his return to the reports.

The viewscreen showed an empty chair, causing Tambu to smile as he leaned toward the mike.

"Tambu here," he announced in carefully modulated tones.

Blackjack appeared on the screen, hurrying to his chair, shirtless and half-hopping as he tried to pull on a pair of pants.

"Sorry, boss," he apologized. "I didn't think you'd answer so fast."

"It's been a slow day," Tambu explained dryly. "What've you got?"

Blackjack hedged. "Well, it might be nothing. But when we dropped in on Trepec here, I picked up a bit of information I thought you should have."

"And that is—" Tambu urged impatiently.

"It seems there's been a run on guns—big ones like we use on our ships."

"Interesting." Tambu frowned. "Any word as to who's been buying?"

"As near as I can find out, they've sold a few each to a lot of planets."

"Strange." Tambu pursed his lips. "Which planets?"

"I've got a list here. Some of 'em are on our subscription list, but most aren't."

"Oh, well," Tambu sighed. "I guess it was bound to happen sometime."

"What's that?"

"The planets are arming themselves," Tambu explained, "though what good they expect ground-mounted guns to be against ships in orbit is beyond me."

"Arming themselves? Against what?"

"Maybe against pirates," Tambu smiled. "But more likely against us. We *have* hit a few planets in our time, you know."

"But that's ridiculous," Blackjack protested. "Ground-mounted guns wouldn't stop us if we decided to hit a planet."

"You know it, and I know it, but apparently the planets don't know it. Oh well, it's their money."

"Are you going to alert the fleet?"

"Why bother?" Tambu yawned. "Any ship of mine that can't hold its own against a ground-mounted attack deserves what they get."

"But if they set up a battery near a spaceport, they might ambush a shuttlecraft," Blackjack cautioned.

"I suppose you're right. All right, give me the list, and I'll pass the word."

He jotted down the names of the planets as Blackjack read them. The list was surprisingly long, between fifteen and twenty planets. Still, it was nothing to worry about.

"Very well, I'll make sure the fleet is warned. Take a couple of extra days while you're there and see if you can find out anything else."

"Right, boss. What are your orders for dealing with one of the planets on the list?"

"I don't know. Hail them from orbit and see what they have to say, I guess. If they make nasty noises, avoid 'em and head for another planet."

"You mean back down?" Blackjack asked.

Tambu smiled at the disappointment in the captain's voice.

"We have to fight often enough already. There's no point in looking for trouble."

"But you said yourself that taking a ground-mounted gun would be no problem," Blackjack argued.

"There are lots of planets, Blackjack. Why whould we risk a ship in a needless brawl, however one-sided, when there are so many that won't put up a fight at all?"

"What if they shoot at us?" Blackjack pressed.

"If you're fired on, you can defend yourself, of course. But under no circumstance will one of my ships fire the first shot. Got it?"

"Affirmative," Blackjack scowled.

"Good enough. Tambu out."

He stared thoughtfully at the blank viewscreen for several moments after signing off. His orders to Blackjack had been rather vague and poorly defined. He'd have to take some time to phrase them better before he sent them out to the fleet. Of course, that would have to wait.

He set the list of planets to one side and turned back to his work table.

Right now he had to wade through these reports. He had stalled long enough—too long. He owed it to the fleet to be selective about his priorities.

INTERVIEW IX

"Though I didn't realize it at the time, that was the start of the Defense Alliance. It never occurred to me that they might be mounting the weapons on ships, much less that they were planning to band together against us."

"That must have been an ugly surprise," Erickson laughed.

There was a moment of silence before the reply came.

"I lost five ships the first day the Defense Alliance began functioning as a unit. The humor of that escapes me."

"I'm sorry," the reporter squirmed. "I didn't know. I didn't mean to make light of it."

"You aren't the only one who didn't know," Tambu sighed. "You see, Mr. Erickson, the Alliance's counteroffensive came before I had gotten around to passing the warning to the fleet."

"So when the Alliance attacked, they were totally unprepared," Erickson finished softly. "I can see where you would feel guilty about that."

"I never like losing a ship, but I don't feel particularly guilty. They were fighting ships and should have been ready for trouble. They fell to attack because the years of low resistance had taken the edge off their alertness."

"But if you had warned them, it might have made a difference," Erickson insisted.

"It might," Tambu admitted. "But I don't think so. Remember that the warning I would have issued would have been against ground installations, not armed ships. One of the things I neglected to mention was that Blackjack's ship was one of those lost on the first day— and he had been warned."

"What happened? Was he caught unaware?"

"Again, the answer is yes and no," Tambu replied. "He saw an armed ship in his vicinity, but he wasn't expecting to be attacked. As a matter of fact, he was on the viewscreen asking me for instructions when the Alliance ship opened fire on him."

"You seem surprisingly unmoved by the memory."

"Do I? That's a strange criticism coming from someone who was just appalled at the Zarn incident."

"Both examples show a callousness to loss of life," the reporter countered.

"True enough," Tambu acknowledged without rancor, "but you must try to see my side of things, Mr. Erickson. In the course of my career I have lost ships, men, and close friends. I feel their loss, but for self-defense I must keep my distance emotionally. If I didn't, I would go insane."

Erickson refrained from comment.

"So the Alliance's threat was felt from the first day on," he said instead.

"You flatter the Alliance with your word choice. The Defense Alliance has never constituted a serious threat to my fleet—then or now."

"But you just said they destroyed five of your ships!"

"Five out of nearly two hundred," Tambu remarked

pointedly. "I'll also admit they've downed several of our ships since—just as we've destroyed several of theirs. I tend to attribute their victories to shortcomings in my own captains rather to any brilliance or competence on their part."

"Excuse my asking, but isn't that a little conceited of you?"

"What's so conceited about acknowledging the weakness of my own fleet?" Tambu asked innocently. "If I wanted to brag, I'd claim that it requires an expert tactician or an ace crew to down one of my ships. The truth is that it's really quite easy to do—if you're faced with a hot-headed captain who won't follow orders."

"I thought your captains followed your orders to the letter," Erickson probed.

"I've never claimed that, Mr. Erickson," Tambu corrected. "In fact, I've given you several examples to the contrary. My captains are human, and they follow popular orders much more strictly than orders they disagree with."

"Then you've issued orders which were unpopular with the fleet?"

"Yes, I have. Orders that were very unpopular."

CHAPTER NINE

Tambu glared at his console viewscreen, fingers tapping his thigh in fierce impatience.

"I would ask that the captains *sit down!*" he ordered in a tone that left no room for rebuttal.

Slowly, the forest of figures on the screen sank back into their chairs—individually, as each captain lost the battle with rebellious indignation.

Tambu waited impatiently until all were seated.

"Put your hands down, too!" he growled dangerously.

Again, the captains complied with grudging hesitancy.

"Very well. I'm going to say this once and once only. This meeting is too large for any vague semblance of democracy. With nearly two hundred of you jammed into one room, I can't even see everyone, much less recognize them to speak."

He paused to wet his lips.

"What is more, even if I could, with this many people

present, simple time parameters dictate that not everyone who wants to speak would be able to."

Mentally he crossed his fingers.

"It is therefore my decision," he announced, "that for the duration of this discussion, I will not recognize speakers from the floor. Instead, I will call upon specific captains whom I feel are most representative of the feelings I have heard expressed over the last several months and let them speak for the fleet."

A low growl of disapproval rose from the assemblage.

"If you are called upon and have nothing to say or feel someone else can say it better," he continued, ignoring the protests, "you may yield the floor to a speaker of your choice. However, independent outbursts or interruptions will not be tolerated. Do I make myself clear?"

A sea of angry eyes glared back at him from the viewscreen, but no one chose to challenge him openly.

"Good." He nodded. "Our first speaker will be Pepe, captain of the *Raven*. Pepe, if you were to be the only speaker for the fleet, how would you describe the current views of the Defense Alliance?"

The swarthy little captain rose slowly to his feet, eyes downcast and brow furrowed as he struggled to organize his thoughts. The crowed waited in patient silence until he was ready to begin.

"The Defense Alliance . . . is not a good thing for us," Pepe managed finally. "We've got a whole bunch of ships there who do nothing—*nothing* but chase us away from planets we're supposed to be protecting. That's bad for business. How are we going to do our jobs if we've always got to be watching the screens for Alliance ships, eh?"

Tambu broke in. "Excuse me for interrupting, Pepe, but how many planets were you patrolling before the Defense Alliance began their operations?"

"Maybe twelve," Pepe answered.

"Your reports say ten. And how many now?"

"Fifteen," Pepe admitted.

"So at least, in your case, your business has increased—not decreased—with the appearance of the Alliance," Tambu observed.

Pepe flushed.

"You told me to speak for the fleet, not my ship," he argued.

"Quite right." Tambu smiled. "Continue."

"What is truly bad," Pepe explained, his voice rising, "is the unhappiness in our crews. For many years now we tell them, 'Practice with your guns . . . be ready to fight.' Now, for the first time we have someone to fight, and we tell them, 'Run away . . . don't fight.' Our crews . . . don't know what to think anymore. They are confused. Are they fighters or runners, eh? We can't keep telling them to be both."

Scattered applause and murmured approval swept the room as Pepe sat down. Tambu pursed his lips and frowned as he watched, then leaned towards the mike.

"Thank you, Pepe. Before we go much further with the discussion, however, we should define our terms. What is this Defense Alliance we're all so concerned about? While most of you know some of the facts, allow me to take a few moments to summarize the information which has come to me, so that we're all on even footing."

There were loud groans and the sound of people shifting in their chairs impatiently, but Tambu ignored them. Despite his awkward speaking form, Pepe had been a little too good at stating the fleet's complaints. Tambu wanted to slow the pace of the meeting before it got out of control.

He began in his best lecturer's monotone; "The Defense Alliance is a collection of some forty ships fielded by the planets with the intent of forming an interstellar peacekeeping force. In this, they are not unlike our own force."

There were mutters of disagreement.

"There are numerous differences, however, which separate the two fleets," he added hastily. "The most obvious is the chain of command on board an individual ship. As you know, many of our ships joined the fleet with crews intact from their previous engagements. The captain and crew are used to working together, and any replacements are selected by the captain."

The crowd was fidgeting, obviously bored by the oration.

"In contrast," Tambu continued, "the Defense Alliance is composed of ships and crews donated by the various planets, and their captains are appointed by the Alliance's High Command—a group which functions independently of any specific planet."

He paused to emphasize his next point.

"This means that the captain and crew of an Alliance ship do not share a common origin, nor do they necessarily agree on methodologies, custom, or tactics. I personally feel this is a major flaw in their organizational logic."

There were more interested faces listening now.

"To emphasize this for a moment, consider how the ships are run. Within our fleet, each ship and ship's captain has autonomy as long as their actions do not go against established policies and guidelines. The High Council of the Defense Alliance, on the other hand, has laid down a strict set of rules as well as a code of conduct which every ship, captain, and crewmember must obey to the letter. Having seen copies of their rules, I can only say that if I tried to get this assembly to abide by them, there would be an armed revolt. The only way the High Council can realistically expect adherence to their rules is if they've crewed their ships with saints and angels."

Laughter greeted this speech, and Tambu began to relax slightly.

"For the rest of it, they are not dissimilar to us. They

finance their fleet with taxes from member planets, taxes which do not vary greatly from the monies paid us by our subscribers. Also, in their effort to form an impartial force, the ships each severed commitments with their planets of origin. As a result, like our fleet, the Defense Alliance answers only to itself—not to any planet or system."

Tambu reviewed his captains on the screen and found them to be calmer and more settled than when he had begun speaking.

"Now that we all understand what we're talking about, let's continue the discussion. Cowboy? Do you have anything to add to what Pepe has already said?"

Tambu had expected that Cowboy would be caught off-balance and would have to flounder while trying to remember Pepe's comments. Instead, the lank Captain surged immediately to his feet and launched into his comments.

"What the Boss sez sums up what we all know," he declared. "We can whip the tar out of them Alliance ships, so what are we running fer? While we're all together for the meeting, Ah think we should take a little extra time and do us some hunting. Ah don't know what the bag limit is on angels an' saints, but Ah bet we could fill it in no time atall!"

Tambu gritted his teeth and rubbed his forehead while the crowd cheered Cowboy. So much for slowing down the pace of the meeting.

"If I understand your logic, Cowboy," he commented dryly after the noise had died down, "you feel that since we can attack and destroy the Alliance fleet, it automatically follows that we should. Is that correct?"

"Well . . . yeah," Cowboy stammered. "Ah guess that's what Ah'm sayin'."

"I see." Tambu smiled. "Then why stop with the Defense Alliance? The fleet's strong enough to totally destroy any planet or system in the universe. After we're done with the Alliance fleet, why not start attacking the planets one by one? We can do it, so why shouldn't we?"

"Yer pokin' fun at me," Cowbody declared, drawing himself proudly erect. "We're supposed to be protectin' the planets, not attackin' them. That's our job."

"Forgive me," Tambu apologized sarcastically. "My mind must be slipping. I wrote the contract we use with the planets, but obviously I've forgotten an important part of that agreement. Could you refresh my memory? Just what part of that agreement says that chasing and destroying the Defense Alliance is part of our job?"

Cowboy dropped his eyes uncomfortably.

"We're—we're supposed to fight against pirates," he murmured lamely.

"Are you saying the Alliance is actually a band of pirates?" Tambu pressed mercilessly. "No one's reported this to me before. That changes everything. Tell me, though, which merchant ships have they attacked? I'll need that information for my records."

Cowboy shook his head silently, not looking up.

"I see," Tambu said at last. "Thank you for your comments, Cowboy. Ratso? Do you have anything to add to the discussion?"

He was careful to use Ramona's fleet name, but her response caught him totally unaware.

"I yield the floor to Captain Egor," she announced without rising.

A murmur of surprise ran through the assemblage. Egor had never spoken before at a captains' meeting.

"Very well," Tambu managed, recovering himself. "Egor?"

The big man rose slowly to his feet and surveyed the room carefully before he spoke. Tambu tried to read the expression on his old friend's face, but found he could not. The only thing he could say for certain was that Egor looked older.

"I'm not as good a talker as most of you," Egor began

hesitantly, "but there's something I've got to tell you about. Something that affects all of us in this room."

He paused for a moment, frowning as if trying to choose his next words.

"Most of you know Whitey," he said at last. "She was captain of the Raven before Pepe. She's an old friend of mine, and I kept in touch with her after she left the fleet and settled on Elei. I've found out . . . well, she's dead."

There was a moment of stunned silence. Then everyone tried to talk at once. Pepe was on his feet, his face pale and drawn, trying to say something to Egor, but his words were lost in the clamor.

Despite his own shock at hearing the news, Tambu's mind was churning with suspicion. Why hadn't Egor informed him of this sooner? More important, why had he chosen now to make his announcement?

Egor was holding his hands up now, motioning for quiet. Slowly, the other conversations subsided as the captains turned to listen.

"What is particularly important," he continued, "is not the fact that Whitey's dead, but rather how she died. The Defense Alliance killed her. One of the Alliance ships visited Elei, and someone told its crew that Whitey used to be with our fleet. They went to her home, dragged her out in the street, and hung her. There was no formal arrest by the Elei authorities, no trial, nothing! Just a lynch mob—a Defense Alliance lynch mob!"

Tambu frowned at the ugly sounds coming from the assembled captains, but Egor wasn't finished yet.

"How do I know?" he called in answer to one of the many questions shouted from the group. "I'll tell you how I know. The Scorpion was there! We were there at Elei!"

His words stilled the rising babble like a bucket of water tossed on a fire. All eyes were on him as he turned to stare at the viewscreen.

"The Scorpion was orbiting Elei when the Alliance

ship arrived," he announced coldly. "Under orders, we withdrew rather than put up a fight. When we returned later, we found out about Whitey."

Tambu bowed his head as the icy rage in Egor's words washed over him. It was obvious that Egor blamed Tambu personally for Whitey's death.

Egor continued, "Unfortunately, my crew heard about it first when they went planetside. I had to exert every bit of discipline and authority at my command to keep them from retaliating against Elei for what the Alliance had done. What's more, I've blocked them from meeting or communicating with the crews from any other ship. It wasn't a popular thing to do, but I felt it was necessary to keep the story from spreading through the fleet before we could discuss it here at the meeting."

Egor faced the other captains, inadvertently turning his back on the viewscreen.

"Well, we're at the meeting now," he growled, "and the question I want to put before the assembled captains is: what are we going to do about it? How long are we going to let the Defense Alliance push us around before we push back?"

A chorus of angry shouts answered his challenge. Tambu gritted his teeth. Egor was showing an unsuspected talent as a rabble rouser. The captains were teetering on the brink of an emotional commitment the fleet could ill afford. Tambu would have to move now if he was to maintain control of the meeting.

"Order!" he barked. "Order, or I'll adjourn the meeting right now! Order!"

Grudgingly, the captains complied. One by one, they returned to their seats, but their faces were tense and expectant as they stared at the viewscreen. Tambu knew they were barely holding their emotions in check. He considered his words carefully.

"Egor," he said after the noise had subsided, "I can only say that I share your grief—as I'm sure all the

captains do. Whitey was liked and respected by all who
knew her, as a captain and a friend."

He paused and took a deep breath before continuing.

"However," he added in a harsher tone, "I must also
say as the chairman of this meeting that what you say
has no bearing at all on the subject under discussion."

Heads snapped up, but he pressed on.

"Whitey was no longer with our fleet, and therefore
outside our sphere of protection. I personally offered to
establish her in a location where her past would be
unknown, but she refused. She chose instead to live
among people who knew her as a fleet captain. She
knew the risk, but make her decision anyway. The fact
that she lost her personal gamble should have no bearing on the policies or decision of the fleet."

The room was staring at him out of the viewscreen,
but no one seemed to be in violent disagreement.

"As such," Tambu concluded, "if you're finished—"

"I'm not finished!" Egor cried.

"Very well," Tambu sighed. "Continue."

"Since you only want to talk about the fleet," Egor
glared, "we will forget about Whitey. Fine. Let's talk
about the *Scorpion* and ships like her who are supposed
to follow your orders. We were driven away from Elei by
an Alliance ship without firing so much as one shot—
following your orders. Speaking for myself, my crew,
and the rest of the fleet, I want to know why. I can accept
not chasing Alliance ships, but why do we have to
run?"

Tambu asked, "When you left Elei, were there other
planets unpatrolled by ships of either fleet?"

"Of course," Egor nodded. "With so many planets
and so few ships, there are always unpatrolled planets."

"Then I'll ask you a question of my own. You ask,
'Why run?' I ask you, 'Why fight?' To protect the planet?
The Alliance won't attack them. To protect yourself?
They never fired a shot at you. To keep the revenues of

the planet? Why bother when there are so many other planets that can replace it?"

Tambu leaned back and sighed.

"What it boils down to, Egor, is that you want to fight because of your pride. You don't want to back down to anyone, anywhere, anytime. That's pride. Now I ask you: do you think it's right to risk not just your life, but your ship and the lives of your crew in a fight that could have been avoided? How much is your pride worth to you?"

Egor flushed and sat down, still angry, but unable to reply.

"Thank you, captain. Now, if we could hear from—"

"I smell a rat!"

There was no mistaking the diminutive figure standing on a chair in the middle of the assemblage.

"I never thought I'd see you climb on a chair to avoid a rat," Tambu observed attempting a joke. "Sit down, A.C."

"I have something to ask," she called back defiantly.

"I said I would not tolerate any outbursts or interruptions, and I meant it! Now sit down!"

A.C. hesitated, then dropped back into her seat.

"Thank you. Now then, Jelly? Would you like to say something at this time?"

The old man half-rose.

"I'd rather yield the floor to Ms. A.C.," he announced.

A titter ran through the group, and Tambu knew he was outmaneuvered.

"Very well," he said politely, trying to salvage his dignity. "A.C.? I believe you had some comments?"

"I have an observation and a question. The observation is that we're being flimflammed! Flimflammed, bamboozled, and hustled! What's more, the one doing the hustling is none other than our own beloved chairman!"

She leveled an accusing finger at the viewscreen, and the assemblage turned to stare.

"No offense, boss," she called. "But I've sat through a lot of these meetings, and I know your style. If this is a free discussion, then I'm Mickey Mouse. You're playing divide-and-conquer games with the meeting, and it's about time you admitted it. By controlling who speaks and in what order, you're choosing what arguments you want to hear and when. Then, after forbidding anyone else to interrupt, you use your position as chair to interrupt as often as you want with questions or observations. You're taking our arguments one at a time and carving them up. That's not your normal style, but that's what you're doing."

She paused for breath.

"Go on," Tambu encouraged, amused despite himself at the accuracy of her statements.

"Well, I've been sitting here trying to figure out why you're doing this, and I can come up with only one answer: Your mind's already made up on the subject of the Defense Alliance. What's more, you don't think that your decision is going to be particularly popular with the captains, so instead of just coming out and speaking your mind, you've set up this cat-and-mouse game. It's my guess you're hoping you can talk us around to where we come up with your idea and think we did it ourselves."

She paused, licked her lips, and continued, her shoulders drooping slightly.

"I don't know. I may be entirely wrong about this, but it's the only thing that fits what's going on. If I'm wrong, I apologize."

Her head came up and her eyes bored out of the viewscreen at him.

"But if I'm right, I think I can speak for all of us when I say could you knock off the bullshit and tell us what you're thinking? You can save everyone a lot of time and emotional stress by just being honest with us. We might not like it, but it beats being treated like children."

She dropped back into her seat, and Tambu winced as

the room stared at the viewscreen, waiting for his answer.

"Thank you, A.C.," he said slowly. "And I really mean that. All I can say is that you're absolutely right."

The captains shifted uneasily and muttered to each other as he continued.

"There are two points of clarification before I share my thoughts with you. First, though I was manipulating the discussion, I was not being close-minded. If a point had been raised from the floor that had escaped my earlier studies on the situation, I would have given it my full consideration. Second, knowing my decision would be unpopular and therefore require considerable explanation, I was trying to bundle that explanation in a choreographed discussion rather than simply lecturing and dictating. Now, I can only apologize to the captains. Whatever my intentions, my methods in dealing with you were less than honest, and therefore in clear violation of my own principles and the spirit of these meetings. I'm sorry. It won't happen again."

He paused for a moment. There was dead silence in the room as the captains waited.

"As to my position on the Defense Alliance, I have given the matter considerable thought and attention. Like all questions, it involves both logic and emotion, and unfortunately my final solution is also logical and emotional.

"As to the logic, I have tried to strip the problem down to the bare essentials. We have always considered ourselves a peacekeeping force. While we will fight to defend our ships or our crews, a peaceful person outside our fleet has nothing to fear from us. The charges and criticisms of us we have attributed to misinterpretation, misinformation, or outright lies.

"The Defense Alliance is also a peacekeeping force. While we seem to be their primary targets, I am sure they would not hesitate to attack a pirate if they chanced upon one. In short, they are in the same business we are—except they aren't as good at it as we are. I'm not talking about fighting here, even though I believe we could beat them man-for-man and ship-for-ship. I'm talking about the day-to-day drudgery once the romanticism wears off. They're all bright-eyed and bushy-tailed, planning to beat us at a game we've been playing for ten years. I don't think they can do it."

He paused for emphasis, scanning the rapt faces in the viewscreen.

"I'm basing my orders—my entire strategy—on that belief. They can't do it. They're going to run into every problem, every financial hassle, every planetside hassle that we did, and I don't think they'll be able to take it! I think they'll fold within a year, two years at most . . . If—and it's a big if—If we don't make a mistake, and right now I think fighting them would be the biggest mistake we could make! If we destory half their fleet, the other half will have a cause to fight for, and we'll never be rid of them. If we destory their whole fleet—"

Tambu rubbed his forehead angrily.

"If we destroy their whole fleet, we'll be making martyrs of them all. The planets will field another fleet, and another—because then we'll have given them proof of what they've been saying all along: that we're gangsters, extortionists who will squash or try to squash anyone who butts in on our territory. That's why I say lean back and wait 'em out. Logically, it's the best plan."

The faces in the screen were mostly thoughtful, though there were several headshakings and scowls.

"That's logically. Emotionally, I feel a bit different."

The tone in his voice brought the heads up as if attached to strings.

"I'm Tambu. I hired and licensed every captain in that room for a peacekeeping force, and as long as my name's on it, that's what it's going to be! That's not subject to debate or a vote—that's the way it is. Period!"

He glared at them. Even though they couldn't see him, they could feel the intensity in his voice.

"Now, each of you signed on voluntarily. I can't force you to stay or to follow my orders. If you and your crews want to go caterwauling across the starlanes chasing the Defense Alliance, fine! Go ahead. You want to demand half of each planet's wealth and your pick of bed-partners? Okay! It's no skin off my nose. You want to gun down every Groundhog who spits in the street when you walk by? Go get 'em! But—"

His voice took on an icy hardness.

"But you aren't going to do it in my name or under the fleet's protection! Whether I command two hundred ships or a hundred . . . or ten, or even one, the weapons at my command belong to a peacekeeping force; and if you cross my path with your games, we'll burn you down like we would any other pirate. For the record and for your information, *that* is my emotional solution, and you're right! It's not going to change!"

He paused and looked at the still, silent figures in the viewscreen.

"Now that that matter's settled," he finished conversationally, "I'll adjourn the meeting for today. Think it over, talk it over. Talk to your crews. Anyone who's leaving can contact me through normal channels to settle their severance pay. For those who are staying, we'll reconvene at 0800 hours tomorrow and see how much of a fleet we have left. Tambu out."

INTERVIEW X

"I take it most of them stayed with the fleet," Erickson observed.

"All of them did. It caused me a bit of concern at the time."

"How so? I should think you would have been pleased that they came around to your way of thinking."

"Perhaps. If I had really believed that I had changed their minds. As it was, I knew that several of the captains were dead set against my plans. If a few ships had left the fleet at that time, I might have been able to kid myself into believing that those remaining were in agreement with me. As it was, I was left knowing that I had serious dissenters in the ranks, and that trouble could flare up at any time."

"And did it?" Erickson urged.

"It did and it does," Tambu answered. "For specific examples, you need only look at your backfile newstapes. Every ship-to-ship battle that's taken place in the last three years has been the result of someone disobeying orders—in one fleet or the other. I repeat my earlier statement: neither the Alliance High Command or I want our ships to fight. We're making a good living from the status quo, and any combat, win or lose, costs too much.''

"But the Alliance was formed to destroy your fleet," the reporter protested.

"They were formed to protect the planets, just as we were," Tambu corrected. "At first they thought they could best do that by destroying us. As I predicted, they found they couldn't do it, and instead settled into a pattern of preventive patrol."

"That last part you didn't actually predict," Erickson pointed out bluntly. "As I recall, your prediction was that they would disband."

"Frankly, I didn't think they would be intelligent enough to adapt," Tambu admitted. "Of course, it's always a mistake to underestimate your opponent. In this case, however, consider it a minor error as it doesn't really matter. The settled universe is big enough for both fleets—particularly now that the Alliance has come to its senses and abandoned its aggressor role.''

"You seem very sure of yourself."

"Do I? Yes, I suppose I do. It's a habit I've gotten into over the years. I often wish I was as confident as I sound.''

"I suppose that's necessary in a command position."

"Quite so. Nothing is as certain to guarantee disaster as if a crew panics—and nothing will panic a crew faster than fear or uncertainty in the leaders over them. The higher you get in the chain of command, the more certain you have to appear. As the head of the fleet, part of my job is to appear infallible."

"Yet you've already admitted your own fallibility."

"There is a great difference between being infallible and seeming infallible, Mr. Erickson. While there is a great pressure on me to be infallible, fortunately, seeming to be infallible is all that is actually required."

Erickson added wryly, "Along with everything else, I must admit that before I had this opportunity to speak with you, I never stopped to think of how grueling your position actually must be. Everything you've told me so far is testimony to the constant demands on your energies and time. What I can't understand is how you stand it. How do you put up with the unending pressure?"

"The answer to that is quite simple, Mr. Erickson," Tambu replied easily. "I don't. To survive unchanged and unscarred would require a superman—and, as I have been trying to assure you, I'm quite human. Often painfully so."

CHAPTER TEN

Ramona awoke alone in Tambu's bed. She groped for his warmth for a few moments, then sleepily burrowed back into her pillow, assuming that he was in the bathroom. Poised on the brink of unconsciousness, her mind registered a small noise on the far side of the cabin. She snuck a lazy peek through her lashes, then blinked her eyes fully open.

The cabin was bathed in a ghostly light, illuminated by the starfield on the console's viewscreen. Silhouetted by the light, Tambu sat naked at the console, staring at the screen.

Ramona frowned as her mind struggled to analyze what she was seeing. This was highly unusual. Occasionally their sleep would be interrupted by a late-night call from a distraught captain, but then Tambu would deal with them in abrupt, terse tones, and return immediately to bed. He slept and loved seldom enough that when he did, he clung to it with an almost savage intensity. He was constantly either engaged in activity or sleeping. Sitting up quietly at night was something new for him.

"What is it, love?" Ramona called, stretching sleepily.

The figure at the console made no move to respond or to acknowledge her question.

"Tambu? Hey!"

Concerned now, she crawled to the foot of the bed and rose, moving to his side.

"Tambu?" she asked again, touching his shoulder lightly.

He turned his head and focused on her as if seeing her for the first time. "Oh! Sorry, love. Did I wake you?"

"What is it?" she pressed, ignoring his question. "Is something wrong?"

"Not really," he shrugged. "I just made a decision, is all. A hard decision."

"A decision? What is it? You haven't said anything about a major decision in the works."

"Believe it or not, I don't tell you everything," he smiled weakly. "No. This is a personal decision, one I've been thinking about for some time now."

"If you're going to tell me, tell me. Otherwise, let's go back to bed."

"Didn't mean to be melodramatic," he apologized. "It's just that it's been a rough decision to make. I didn't want to—I'm doing it again."

He ran a hand through his hair, then raised his gaze to look her squarely in the eye.

"You see, I've decided to retire. I'm going to step down as head of the fleet."

Ramona stared at him, started to speak, then sank down in a chair shaking her head.

"I—I'm sorry, love," she managed at last. "You caught me off guard. This is kind of sudden."

"Not for me," Tambu proclaimed grimly. "It's been on my mind for a long time now."

"Then you're serious?" Ramona asked incredulously, still trying to deal with his statement in her own mind. "You're really going to retire?"

He nodded slowly.

"I've got to. I've been seesawing back and forth for years, but now I don't even think I've got a choice anymore."

There was something in the tone of his voice—something new. Her shock at his decision was swept aside by a wave of concern for his well-being.

"Do you want to talk about it?" she offered gently.

For several moments he didn't respond; then he turned back to her with a sigh.

"I suppose I should. A lot of people are going to be asking a lot of questions when I make my decision public. I might as well get some practice explaining in advance."

He lapsed into silence again, frowning and pursing his lips. Ramona waited patiently.

"You know, it's funny," he said at last with a nervous smile. "I've been thinking about this so long, I could go through the problem in my sleep, but now that I've got to verbalize it, I don't know where to start."

"I'm not going anywhere," Ramona soothed, drawing her legs up under her. "Take your time and start anywhere."

"Well," he sighed. "For openers, look at this."

He extended a hand at chest height, fingers spread loosely.

Ramona peered at it, but saw nothing unusual. She shot a cautious glance at him and found him frowning at his hand.

"That's funny," he mused to himself. "A while ago, it was shaking like a leaf. I couldn't stop it."

"I know," Ramona nodded.

"I've seen it before," she explained. "When you were sleeping. Sometimes you'd lie there shaking all over. I always thought it was fatigue from pushing yourself so hard. You know how sometimes I nag you about getting more sleep? Well, that's why. I get really worried about you."

"I get worried about me, too," Tambu acknowledged. "But it goes a lot deeper than fatigue. It's the main reason I'm quitting."

He paused again. Ramona waited.

"I'm tired, love," he said softly. "Not just physically, get-some-sleep tired, I mean tired all the way through. I'm tired of making decisions, tired of giving orders, tired of speaking out, tired of not speaking out. . . tired of being Tambu."

"I'd say you've got a problem," Ramona observed with mock judiciousness. "I mean, when Tambu gets tired of being Tambu, where does that leave the fleet?"

"I'll let you in on a deep, dark secret, Ramona," Tambu announced wearily. "Perhaps the most closely guarded secret in the fleet."

He looked over both shoulders with melodramatic suspicion, then leaned forward to whisper in her ear.

"You see, I'm not Tambu."

"Really?" Ramona gasped, mimicking his manner. "Well, while I am shocked and horrifed, I must compliment you sir, on your excellent impersonation. You look, talk, walk, drink and make love just like him. I never would have guessed if you hadn't revealed yourself."

"I'm serious," he replied with no trace of levity. "I'm not Tambu."

Ramona studied him thoughtfully for a moment.

"Okay, I'll play your game. If you aren't Tambu, who are you?"

"I'm a space bum," he announced. "A space bum who had an idea to get himself and his friends out of a bad situation. Part of the idea—a very small part—was to take on an assumed name: Tambu. By itself, the new name created no problems. But them something happened. The space bum and his friends—and a few new friends—decided to build a mythical figure around the name Tambu. You remember, love. You were there at the time."

Ramona nodded dumbly.

"It was ridiculously easy to do," he continued. "We've been conditioned by literature, Tri-D adventures, and other entertainment forms to recognize a heroic figure. All we had to do was provide a few high points and hide any contradictory information, and people would complete the picture themselves. They would see Tambu as a powerful, omnipresent, charismatic leader they could trust and follow. He must be! Otherwise, why is everybody else following him?"

Ramona dropped her eyes and gnawed on her lip. She looked up again as Tambu laid a gentle hand on her arm.

"Don't feel bad, love," he chided. "You didn't force me into anything I didn't want to do. It was a con game, and one I went along with willingly. Why not? It was fun. It was kind of like having the lead in a play, and I played my role to the hilt."

He leaned back again, his expression becoming more serious.

"The trouble is, the play never ended," he said in a low voice. "We never had the curtain call, when the players came out onstage and said 'Hey, look! We're just actors. What you've seen is just make-believe made momentarily plausible by master illusionists.' Because we've never clarified our position, the audience has accepted the illusion as reality, and by that acceptance made it reality."

"Slow up a little, love," Ramona said, shaking her head. "You lost me on that last curve."

"Let me try it from a slightly different angle. Any actor or con artist—or even a salesman—will tell you that to be successful, you have to believe what you're doing. Well, to be Tambu, I had to project myself into that character. I kept asking myself, 'What would a powerful person do in this situation?' 'What would a charismatic leader say to that problem?' I did that for years, until Tambu became more familiar to me than my own character. I got so I could do Tambu without thinking, purely by reflex. Do you see what I'm saying? I became Tambu, but Tambu isn't me!"

"I see your point," Ramona acknowledged. "But couldn't you also say Tambu is just another phase of your own development? I mean, I don't think you've done anything as Tambu that you would have been morally against in your earlier life. In a lot of ways, he's simply a projection of yourself."

"I don't know anymore," Tambu sighed. "And that's why I feel I've got to get out. Lately I find myself saying and doing things as Tambu that go completely against my grain. If I keep going, I'm afraid I'll lose myself to him completely."

"What things went against the grain? Just to satisfy my curiousity."

"Little things, mostly. But things that bother me. Remember the last captains' meeting? When Egor told us about Whitey getting killed. Part of me—the original me—wanted to get sick when I heard that. I wanted to walk away from the screen and hide for a couple of days—cry, get drunk, anything to ease the pain I felt. I mean, in a lot of ways, Whitey was like the sister I never had. She was patient, critical, supportive—more than a friend to me in every way. When I found out she was dead, and how she died, it hit me hard. So what did I do? I gave her a one-line eulogy and then told everyone her death didn't matter. That wasn't me talking, that was Tambu. Our opinions and reactions differed, and his won."

"But you were trying to make a point," Ramona argued. "An important point about not fighting the Defense Alliance. Not only was the news of Whitey's death distracting, it could have undermined your arguments by raising emotions against the Alliance. You should take that into consideration."

"Should I?" Tambu smiled. "You know that original me I keep talking about? You know what he felt about the whole matter? He was with the captains! He wanted to go out there and smash the bastards in the Alliance and anyone else who dared to take up arms against us. That's what he wanted, but Tambu wouldn't allow it, just like he wouldn't let the captains go off half-cocked. That's the rest of my problem. I can't ease off on Tambu, let him develop into what I was originally. The fleet needs Tambu—a cold mind with an eye for the overview. If I let the original me—the one I'm fighting to save—take over the fleet, it would be disastrous. I've got to make the choice: either stay with the fleet as Tambu, or save myself and leave."

"Your concern for the fleet is touching," Ramona drawled sarcastically. "What happens to the fleet if you retire? You'll be leaving a lot of friends holding the bag."

"What friends?" Tambu challenged. "With the exception of you, I don't have any friends left in the fleet. Puck, Whitey, even Blackjack, whom I never really liked, all of them are gone. Everyone else knows me as an authoritative voice on a blank viewscreen."

"There's Egor," Ramona reminded him.

Tambu thought for a moment, then sighed.

"I suppose you're right," he admitted. "Egor and I are still friends, even though we haven't gotten along too well lately. I still cover for him, and he still tries to be captain for me. It must be friendship. There's no other reason for it."

"But everyone else can go hang—if you'll pardon the pun. You must be a different person. That doesn't sound like Tambu at all."

Tambu slumped back in his chair, his eyes downcast, but his hands balled into tight fists.

"You're wrong, Ramona," he said quietly. "I *do* care what happens to the fleet. That's my problem. If I didn't care, I could just take a shuttle down at the next planet, and never look back. I do care, though, so I've been racking my brain trying to think of a way to have my cake and eat it, too. I want to be able to save myself for myself, and at the same time ensure the fleet's continued survival."

"That's a pretty tall order," Ramona said. "I don't see any way you could do it."

"I've figured a way," Tambu said quietly. "If I hadn't, I wouldn't be retiring. The fleet means a lot to me. I wouldn't sell it down the river just to save myself."

"That sounds more like the Tambu I know," Ramona said eagerly. "What's the plan? I'm all ears."

"Well . . . not *all* ears," Tambu smiled, leaning forward to caress her lightly.

"Stop that!" She slapped his hand. "You'll get me all distracted, and I want to hear this master plan of yours."

"See what I mean about my job getting in the way of my personal life?" Tambu sighed in mock dejection.

"Are you going to tell me the plan or not?"

"Well, I got the idea from an item on the agenda for the next captains' meeting," Tambu began.

"Swell! I haven't seen a copy of the agenda yet."

"I know. I haven't distributed them yet."

"Tell me the plan!"

Tambu yawned. "As I was saying before I was interrupted, there is an item on the agenda calling for the formation of a Captains Council. The general idea is to select a dozen or so captains, each of whom will meet with small groups of ships throughout the year. Then, at the yearly meeting, they will represent the ships in the policy arguments with me. It's an attempt to avoid mob scenes like last year's meeting when there were too many captains, all trying to talk at once on every subject."

"Will the other captains be allowed to attend, too?" Ramona asked.

"I don't know. Hopefully, there would be enough trust in the Council that it wouldn't be necessary for the other captains to sit in. It wouldn't surprise me, though, if they insisted on attending for the first few years until that trust was built."

"What has this got to do with your plan?" Ramona pressed.

"Isn't it obvious?" Tambu blinked. "That Council could take over as the governing body of the fleet after I'm gone."

"Do you think the fleet will go along with that?" Ramona asked. "I mean, everybody's used to having one person at the top. I'm not sure they'll like switching over to rule by committee."

"I think the fleet would be better off with a council calling the shots. If you put all the weight on one person, there's too much chance that he'll fold—or worse, abuse the power. If they really want one person at the controls, though, I suppose they could choose one or let the Council choose one."

"Anyone specific in mind?" Ramona asked.

"If I had to name my successor or make a recommendation," Tambu frowned, "I'd have to go with A.C. She's shrewd as well as intelligent, and gutsy enough for three people."

"She also has a temper that won't quit," Ramona observed dryly.

"Nobody will be ideal. I'm hoping that the added responsibility would calm her down."

"There is one person who's ideal," Ramona suggested.

"Who's that?"

"You," Ramona said bluntly. "Face it, love, you in-

vented the job and defined its range and parameters. No
matter who gets picked, nobody's going to be better at
being Tambu than Tambu."

"But I've told you how I feel about that," he protested.

"Yes, you have," Ramona retorted. "Now let me tell
you how the fleet will feel. The captains will feel betrayed, abandoned, and shat upon. They're in the fleet
because they believe in you and you believe in what
you're doing. How do you think they'll feel when you
try to take that away from them? I say 'try,' because I'm
not sure they'll let you step down."

"How will they stop me—kill me?" Tambu laughed
sardonically. "That's what it would take, and either
way, they won't have Tambu at the controls anymore.
No, hopefully they'll realize that if I'm not working
willingly, I'll be no good to them at all."

"That's if they're thinking logically, which they don't
always do," Ramona retorted. "At the very least, a lot of
people are going to try to talk you out of it."

"I know. One of the things I don't know yet is how and
when I'm going to make the announcement—if at all.
It'll blow things wide open if I do it at the captains'
meeting. Ideally, I'd like to wait until the Council idea
has been passed and the members chosen, then tell them
in a private meeting. That would give me some time to
work with them, train them, and help organize the new
structure before I left. I'll just have to wait and see what
the temperature of the water is like at the meeting before
I make up my mind on that. Maybe it would be easier to
just establish the structure and then dissappear—you
know, missing in action. They can't argue with me if
they can't find me."

"Well, I can't see any way you can make a popular
move," Ramona said. "If you let the captains in on your
decision, they'll turn on you like a pack of animals."

"So what's new?" Tambu smiled. "I've gotten used to
it over the last couple years. You know, Ramona, lately

I've taken to seeing the captains as opponents rather than allies. They're a force to be dealt with—and they scare me more than the Defense Alliance ever could. If the Alliance starts getting frisky, I've got the fleet to fight them with. If the captains get upset, though, it's just me and them. No one's going to intercede in my behalf."

Ramona was silent for a few moments.

At last she sighed, "If that's how you see things, it's probably just as well if you step down. One question, though. You've already made it clear you don't think I could step into your position and run the fleet. What do you think my chances would be of getting a spot on the Council?"

"You?" Tambu blinked. "But you . . . I'm sorry. I've been so busy talking about myself, I haven't said anything about my other plans. I was hoping you'd come with me when I left."

Ramona gnawed her lip for a moment.

"Thanks for the invitation," she said finally. "Listening to you talk, I wasn't sure I'd be welcome. Now, at least, I know I've got a choice."

"But will you come with me?"

"I—I don't know," Ramona admitted. "So much of what I love in you is tied into the fleet. I mean, I love Tambu—and what you've been telling me is you're not Tambu, that you're someone else. I don't know that other person. I'm not sure if I'd love you more or hate you."

"I had counted on your coming along," Tambu said softly.

"Would it change your decision if I said I wouldn't go with you?" Ramona asked.

Tambu looked at her for a long moment, then lowered his eyes and shook his head.

"Then I'll have to think about it," Ramona sighed. "Come back to bed now. I'll give you my answer before you leave the fleet."

INTERVIEW XI

"Did Ramona's argument surprise you? About your being the only one who could run the fleet?"

"I felt it was exaggerated. There is a natural tendency in any group to feel that the current leader is the only one who can hold things together—particularly if that leader is the one who formed the group originally. A more realistic attitude is found in business, where they maintain that no one is irreplaceable."

"There it is again," the reporter murmured.

"I beg your pardon?"

"Hmmm? Sorry, I was just thinking out loud. It's just that throughout the interview, in all your examples, you seem to downplay yourself as a charismatic figure. It's as if you feel that anyone could do what you've done, if given the opportunity."

"In many ways, you're correct, Mr. Erickson. For a long time I saw myself as nothing more than an opportunistic space bum who got lucky. I didn't consider myself a charismatic figure so much as a weak leader who was scrambling desperately trying to live up to the faith and trust that others had placed in him. I didn't control or manipulate circumstances, they controlled me. I dealt with situations as they arose in the manner I thought best at that time. It's been only recently that I've begun to realize how exceptional one must be to do the job I've done. That's what's given me my confidence, but it had to be built slowly over my entire career. I didn't start with it."

"So at the time you considered retiring, you still felt that any one of a number of people could run the fleet, once you turned your files over to them?" the reporter guessed.

"That is correct. Aside from the fact that I had designed the job, I didn't see why I should be singled out to serve. While a new leader would have doubtless handled things differently, I was confident that the position was transferable."

"You were just going to walk away from it?" Erickson marveled. "The power, the notoriety, everything? Just up and leave it?"

"That's correct. And believe me, the decision was every bit as hard as it sounds. You see, I *like* being Tambu. That's one thing that was not mentioned in that conversation. There is something giddy and addictive about having a roomful of powerful people hanging on your every word, waiting for your commands or pronouncements."

"And, of course, there's always the detail of having the power of life and death over a vast number of people," the reporter added.

"Unfortunately, yes. It's at once appealing and horrifying. I feel it speaks highly of me that I could have seriously planned to give it up."

"I assume you changed your mind again after the mood passed." Erickson smiled.

"It was more than a mood. And it wasn't the lure of power that made me change my plans."

"Did Ramona talk you out of it, then?"

"No, she didn't even try."

"Then the captains must have raised sufficient protest—"

"Mr. Erickson," Tambu interrupted, "I think you fail to realize the strength of my will. Once my mind was made up, no person or group of people could have changed it. When the yearly meeting was convened, I had every intention of carrying out my plan."

"Yet you are still obviously in command of the fleet. When you made your announcement, something must have happened to change your plans."

"As a matter of fact," Tambu reminisced softly, "the subject never came up."

CHAPTER ELEVEN

Tambu watched silently as the captains gathered for the yearly meeting. For nearly an hour now he had been sitting in front of his viewscreen, watching and listening.

Other years, he had waited until the signal came for the meeting ship that the captains were assembled and ready before activating his screen to call the group to order. Usually, his last hours before the meeting were filled with activity as he organized his notes, reviewed personnel files, and made last-minute additions to his plans for the upcoming year.

This year was different. This year, he had been watching the room when the first captains appeared and helped themselves to the coffee provided by the host crew. This year, he studied each of the captains as they entered the meeting room, observing their expression and body tension, noting whom they chose to talk with prior to the meeting.

His spying was born of nervousness and anxiety over

the course of today's meeting. He wanted the Council motion to pass—smoothly if possible—but if need be, he was ready to bend a few people to push it through. If the motion didn't pass, it would delay his retirement until an alternate system could be devised and approved.

The captains would probably raise their eyebrows if they knew how closely they were being scrutinized, but the odds of them finding out were slim to nonexistent. Only Tambu and Egor knew he was watching, and Egor could be trusted to keep the secret. That was partially the reason he had chose the *Scorpion* as the site for this year's meeting. The other reason was that he wanted to provide one final public display of his approval of Egor, hopefully to end once and for all the criticisms of his friend which abounded in the fleet.

He wondered for a moment if Egor would resign once he learned of Tambu's plans, but dismissed the thought. Egor's reaction, like those of the other captains, would be apparent soon enough when he made the announcement. Until then, it was a waste of mental energy to try to second guess what would happen.

His attention turned again to the figures on the screen. For the first time in years he viewed them as individuals rather than as business associates. A lot of his hopes were riding on the people in that room. He had picked them, trained them, argued with them, and bled with them. Could they hold the fleet together after he was gone? If anyone could, they could. There would be some changes, of course—possibly even some major policy revisions. Still, they were experienced captains, and he was confident they would rise to the challenge.

Egor came forward, moving toward the screen. He had been standing by the door, greeting each captain and checking them off on the master list as they arrived. The fact that he had abandoned his post signaled that all were in attendance now. The captains knew that, too, and began drifting toward their seats as Egor began working the viewscreen controls.

A blinking red light appeared on Tambu's console, the ready signal. He paused for a moment, looking at the expectant assemblage. This was the fleet! His creation! Realization came to him that this would be the last time he would deal with them, command them as a unit.

With leaden slowness, he leaned toward the mike. "Good morning. I trust everyone is well rested and ready for a full day's business?"

Assorted groans and grimaces greeted his words. This had come to be a traditional opening. He knew, as they did, that the yearly meetings had become a week-long social gathering and party for the crews. That, combined with the captains' own last-minute preparations, usually guaranteed that no one arrived at the meeting well rested.

"Before we begin," he continued, "I'd like to take a moment to thank Captain Egor and the *Scorpion's* crew for hosting this year's meeting. As those of you who have hosted these meetings in the past will testify, there's a lot of work that goes into the preparations. Egor?"

Egor rose to a round of automatic applause, and gestured for silence.

"My crew has asked me to convey their regrets and apologies to you for their absence from the pre-meeting parties on board the other ships," he announced with pompous formality. "Contrary to popular belief, this is not because I've confined to the ship."

Egor paused for a moment, but no laughter greeted his attempted joke.

"Actually," he continued, "they've been working on their own on a surprise they've cooked up for today's meeting. I don't know what it is, but they've been planning it ever since they found out the yearly meeting was going to be on the *Scorpion*—and if I know my crew, it should be memorable."

He sat down, and Tambu waited until the polite applause died.

"Thank you, Egor. Now, before we get into the agenda, I'd like to announce a change in policy as to how this meeting is to be conducted. As you recall, last year we encountered difficulty discussing points on the agenda, both from the size of the assemblage, and from my attempting to guide the discussion from the chair. Well, this year, we're going to try something different."

A low murmur rose at this, but most of the captains listened in rapt attention.

"This year, we will have a captain conduct the discussion from the floor of the meeting. If I have something to say, I'll have to wait my turn with the rest of you. In an effort to maintain complete impartiality, I have assigned a different captain to each item on the agenda. These captains were chosen at random, and their names subsequently withdrawn from the pool until every captain has conducted a discussion."

The murmur rose to a buzz as the captains discussed the announcement. As Tambu had predicted, most of the reactions were favorable.

"Now, then," Tambu said after the captains had quieted down, "I believe we're ready to start on the agenda. The first item is a proposal for a Council of Captains to replace or supplement the yearly meetings. Captain Ratso, will you conduct the discussion, please?"

The random selection of captains had been a white lie. Tambu had specifically chosen Ramona to conduct this first discussion and had briefed her carefully as to how it was to be done. He had two very important reasons for doing this. First, her handling of the discussion would set the pattern for the other discussion leaders to follow. More important, this item would be the key for his smooth retirement, and he wanted it handled carefully. While Ramona hadn't given him her answer yet whether or not she would accompany him when he left, she was as eager as he to be sure that his departure was handled with a minimum of hassle on all fronts.

"Thank you, Tambu," Ramona said, taking her place at the front of the room. "This item could have a major effect on all of us. I think we are in agreement that these meetings are getting too large to handle the problems that arise each year. We need an alternative to the mass yearly meetings to conduct our business. The question is, is this proposal the best solution? A.C.? Would you start the discussion please?"

Tambu smiled to himself as A.C. clambered onto her chair. Ramona was following his instructions to the letter. A.C. was one of the best shotgunners at the meeting, lying back quietly until everyone had committed themselves to an opinion, then cutting the legs out from under them. By setting her up to speak first, Ramona was ensuring that A.C. would be the one on the defensive instead of having the final shot.

"I don't think we need a Captain's Council at all," A.C. declared loudly. "In fact, before this item appeared on the agenda, I was going to move that we abolish the yearly meetings altogether."

An angry snarl greeted this suggestion. Tambu rocked back and forth in his chair gleefully. This was better than he had hoped. A.C.'s abrupt negativism was setting the assembly against her. That meant they would be that much more receptive to a positive proposal.

"Grow up, people!" A.C. was shouting at her decriers. "Can't you accept the facts? Didn't the boss spell it out for you last year? The captains have no power at all—we're paper dragons. Tambu calls the shots, and his word is final. All we do is provide background noise. He lets us get together and talk and argue so we'll think we've got a say in what's going on, but it doesn't really matter. He gives the orders and that's that."

She turned to face the front of the room, and for a moment Tambu had the uncomfortable feeling she could see him through the screen.

"Don't get me wrong, boss. I'm not complaining. I

think you're doing a terrific job of running the show. You're fair, you're careful, and you have a better feel for what's going on in the fleet than any five or ten or twenty of us put together. Now, I don't pretend I agree wholeheartedly with all your decisions, particularly when they're shoved down my throat. In the long run, though, I've got to admit you've been right. If I didn't feel that way, I wouldn't still be with you—and neither would anyone else in this room. You're the boss, and I wouldn't have it any other way."

Tambu writhed before this display of loyalty. Without knowing it, A.C. had voiced a strong argument against his retirement. It stood as a grim warning of what he could expect when he made his announcement.

"I hate to interrupt, A.C.," Ramona said, "but you're supposed to be giving your views on the proposal on the floor."

"You want my views?" A.C. snarled. "I'll give you my views. I think a Council of Captains would be a waste of time. I think these meetings are a waste of time, and a Council would only compound it. I think we should quit wasting our time and let Tambu get on with his business of running the fleet."

She sat down to a rising tide of protests. Clearly her speech was not popular with the other captains.

"I'd like to reply to that, if I might," Tambu interjected his voice through the din.

"I'm sorry, boss," Ramona apologized, "there are a couple of speakers ahead of you. Remember, it was your rule!"

A ripple of laughter greeted this, mixed with a few catcalls. But Tambu was not upset. Things were still going according to plan. Ramona had agreed that he should try to interrupt after the first speaker, only to be blocked by the discussion leader. It provided a bit of comic relief, while at the same time setting a precedent for later discussions. Top man or not, Tambu was not to be allowed to interrupt at will. More important, the discussion leader could stop him without fear of repercussions.

"Jelly?" Ramona was saying. "Would you care to speak next?"

Tambu frowned slightly as the old man rose to his feet. He wouldn't have chosen Jelly to speak next. The aging captain was still sharp enough mentally, not to mention highly respected, but he tended to be deathly slow when speaking. The pace of the meeting was bound to suffer with Jelly's speaking so early. Still, he was Ramona's choice, and Tambu was going to have to get used to things being handled differently during these discussions.

"I must take exception to Captain A.C.'s comments," Jelly was saying. "These meetings serve several functions, one of which is to force the captains to hear each other. When we do, we find that our views and opinions are shared by many others, and it becomes unnecessary for each of us to speak. This avoids repetition, and saves Tambu the trouble of hearing the same suggestion or complaint forty or fifty times."

He paused to clear his throat, coughing slightly.

"Excuse me. As to the Cpatains' Council," he continued, "this is also something which could potentially save us considerable time. If for example, a problem—"

He broke off suddenly, coughing hard and clutching at his chair for support.

Tambu bolted upright, staring at the screen as the room dissolved into chaos. He reached for his mike—but before he could speak, the viewscreen went blank.

He froze, blinking at the screen in disbelief. This was impossible! Communications equipment simply didn't break down. In the years of the fleet's existence, there had never been a failure of communications gear—on any ship.

Moving quickly, Tambu punched out a familiar com-

bination of buttons and a view of immediate space filled
with the ships of the fleet sprang to life on the screen.
That gave him some assurance. At least the problem
wasn't with his gear. Something must be malfunction-
ing with the equipment on the *Scorpion*. Strange that it
should happen just as there was a disruption in the
meeting . . . or was it a coincidence?

Tambu frowned, trying to reconstruct the scene in his
mind. Had Jelly been the only one coughing? He had a
flashing impression of people moving away from Jelly
during the commotion—not towards him, as would be
the normal reflex.

Shaking the thought from his mind, Tambu made a
few adjustments to his controls and tried the *Scorpion*
again.

"Calling the *Scorpion!* This is Tambu. Come in,
Scorpion."

To his relief, the response was almost immediate. The
display, however, was not of the captains' meeting.
Instead, there was a bearded man on the screen with a
tangle of dark, unkempt, shoulder-length hair. Tambu
noted several features in the cabin behind the man, and
realized he was in Egor's private quarters.

"*Scorpion* here, sir," the man announced. "We've
been expecting your call."

Tambu did not recognize the man immediately and
there was something in his tone which hinted of disre-
spect. But the situation was too pressing to prolong the
conversation.

"If you're expecting my call," he snapped, "then you
probably know what's going wrong. Assign someone to
repair the viewscreen in the meeting room immediately.
Tell Captain Egor to declare a recess until the screen is
functioning. Then have him report to me."

"There's nothing wrong with the viewscreen in the
meeting room," the man informed him tensely. "We
deliberately overrode the transmission."

A flash of anger shot through Tambu.

"We?" he barked. "Who is 'we,' and by what authority do you—"

"We are the crew of the Scorpion," the man interrupted. "And it is my pleasure to inform you that we've just taken control of the ship."

Tambu's mind reeled. A mutiny! Devishly well timed, too!

Almost without thinking, his hand activated the computer tie-in to the console, seeking the identity of his adversary in the fleet's personnel files. The search was thankfully brief, and the information appeared on a small supplemental data screen.

"I see," he said quietly, hiding his agitation. "Tell me, Hairy . . . it is Hairy, isn't it? With an 'i'? Just what do you and your friends hope to accomplish with this takeover? You're completely boxed in by the fleet, you know. I don't see much chance of your escaping."

"We—we just want a fair deal," Hairy stammered, visibly shaken by Tambu's recognition.

"A fair deal?" Tambu frowned. "You'll have to be a little clearer than that, Hairy. I was under the impression you already had a fair deal."

"Maybe that's what you call it," Hairy snarled, his nervousness overcome by his anger. "But we don't see it that way."

"Don't you think this is a bit extreme?" Tambu chided him. "There are formal channels for registering complaints. I fail to see why you feel you have to resort to such drastic methods to make your feelings known."

"Normal channels!" The man spat. "Normal channels haven't been open to us. That's one of our complaints. Our last petition to the captain got torn up in front of us. When we've tried to complain to you, either the captain hasn't relayed the messages, or you've ignored them completely."

Memories flooded Tambu's head. Memories of Egor's

numerous calls, assaulting him with tales of his crew's discontent. Memories of Tambu telling him to handle it himself.

"We've even tried complaining to crews from other ships when we met them," Hairy continued. "We told them to pass the word to their captains, hoping it would reach you indirectly. That didn't get us anything but more grief when the other captains called Egor to criticize his handling of his crew."

"If the situation is as bad as that, why don't you just resign?" Tambu asked.

"Resign?" Hairy snorted. "Cheese tried to resign. The captain killed him outright. After that, no one's tried to resign. We don't get leave planetside anymore, so we don't even have a chance to jump ship."

"When was Cheese killed?" Tambu demanded. "I don't recall seeing a report on that."

"The captain reported it as a suicide, and of course, no one thought to question his word."

"So you devised this trick to get my attention," Tambu observed grimly. "When you plan a surprise for the captains, you don't kid around, do you?"

"We figured since you only listen to the captains, the best way for us to be heard was to come between you and them," Hairy sneered. "You want to see how your captains' meeting is going?"

The man leaned forward, reaching for his console's controls. Immediately the screen changed to display the Scorpion's meeting room. The captains were sprawled all over the room, some crumpled on the floor, others slumped in their chairs. No one was moving.

"There are your precious captains," Hairy taunted, reappearing on the screen. "Amazing what a couple of canisters of knockout gas in the vent system can do, isn't it? All of them, sleeping like babies inside of thirty seconds."

"You think that by holding the captains hostage, you

can force me to let you and your shipmates leave the fleet?" Tambu asked levelly.

"You've got us all wrong," Hairy protested. "We don't want to leave the fleet. If that was what we wanted, we could have jumped the captain anytime and just sailed away. No, we've talked to enough of the other crews to know the *Scorpion* has been the exception, not the rule in your fleet. We're willing to stay in the fleet—once we get a few of our differences resolved."

"Very well," Tambu sighed. "If you revive the captains and allow them to finish their meetings, I'll extend immunity to you from reprisals. Furthermore, I'll give you my promise to personally look into the situation on board the *Scorpion* at my earliest possible convenience. Agreed?"

"Not agreed!" Hairy shot back, shaking his head violently. "You aren't going to deal with us 'at your earliest convenience.' You're going to deal with us right now. What's more, the captains aren't going anywhere until after we've settled this. You don't seem to understand. We're dealing from a position of power. You don't tell us what to do, we tell you!"

His words hung in the air, forever irretrievable. Unseen by Hairy, Tambu's eyes narrowed, and his expression froze into icy grimness.

"Is that how it is?" he said softly. "And just what sort of orders do you and your pirates have in mind for me?"

Any of the captains could have told Hairy that when Tambu's voice went quiet like that, it was a clear danger signal. What's more, the men never wanted Tambu to think of them as pirates. Unfortunately, the captains weren't there to advise Hairy at the moment.

"Well," Hairy began confidently, "first we demand the right to choose our own captain. Even though we'll probably elect him from within our own crew, we want copies of your personnel files to see who else might be available and what their qualifications are. Second, we

think the crews should have as much say in how the fleet is run as the captains do . . . including access to you for private conferences. Finally, we want your signature on an order to execute Egor for gross abuse of the authorities of a captain."

"Is that all?" Tambu asked mildly.

"Well, there are a lot of little things," Hairy admitted. "We each want a bonus to compensate us for what we've had to put up with serving under Egor—and there are some benefits we think every crewman in the fleet should have. We're still putting the list together. We figure we should make the most of this while we've got the chance."

"What chance?" Tambu pressed.

"The chance to call the shots for a change. If we set this up right, we can have a hand in all decisions from here on."

"And if I don't agree, you'll kill the captains," Tambu said slowly.

"You understand perfectly," Hairy leered. "You don't really have much of a choice, do you?"

"I have a few." Tambu smiled. "There is one thing I don't understand, though. I think you may be laboring under a misconception. Who do you think you're talking to right now?"

"Who?" Hairy blinked, taken aback by the question. "This is Tambu, isn't it? I mean, you said—"

"That's right, sonny!" Tambu exploded, his voice cracking like a whip. "You're talking to Tambu! Not some sweaty planetside official who wets his pants when you rattle your saber. I'm Tambu, and nobody tells me how to run my fleet. Not the planets, not the Defense Alliance, not the captains, and definitely not some jackass who's throwing a tantrum because he thinks he's being treated badly."

"But if you—" Hairy protested.

"You think you're in a position of power?" Tambu

snarled, ignoring the interruption. "Sonny, you don't know what power is. I'd give orders to burn an entire planet to cinders, people and all, before I'd let you blackmail me into turning the fleet over to you, and you try to bargain with a roomful of hostages? You're a fool, Hairy! If my mother was in that room, I wouldn't lift a finger to save her."

Hairy's face was pale in the viewscreen. He no longer looked arrogant and confident. He looked scared.

"If you try anything, we'll open fire on the fleet. There are a lot of ships in range of the *Scorpion's* guns, and their crews are all busy partying. We could do a lot of damage before we went down."

The fleet! Tambu's mind raced as he searched his memory for the deployment of the ships around the *Scorpion*. There were none lying close to the mutineers' ship, but over half a dozen within the maximum range of its weapons. They were too far out to muster a boarding party before the *Scorpion* could bring its guns to bear. What's more, now that he was in contact with the mutineers, there was no way he could alert the fleet or order the endangered ships to disperse without Hairy's knowing he was planning something.

Still, he couldn't surrender control of two hundred ships to save six ships any more than he could do it to save one ship—one ship!

Slowly, his hand released the double lock on one of the levers on his console.

"Hairy," Tambu said coldly. "You just made a big mistake, Hairy. I was willing to listen to your complaints because I think you've got a valid case. But I can't be nice to you anymore, Hairy. You just became a danger to the fleet."

Hairy was panicky now. He wet his lips and tried to speak, but nothing came out.

"Look at the console in front of you, Hairy. Do you see the red lever? The one with the double safety lock? Do you know what that is, Hairy?"

"It's—it's the ship's self-destruct mechanism," Hairy managed at last.

"That's right, Hairy. But did you know I can activate that mechanism from right here at my console? Did you know that, Hairy?"

Hairy shook his head woodenly.

"Well, you know it now! Game time is over, Hairy. You have five seconds to call your crew to assemble in front of that screen where I can see them all, or I activate the mechanism."

Despite his firm declaration, Tambu was holding his breath, hoping. If the mutineers would only comply now—stand there so he could see they weren't manning the guns, leveling their sights on an unsuspecting fleet—

For a moment, Hairy wavered. Sweat beaded on his forehead and his eyes darted to someone off-screen. Another voice called out, its words indistinguishable, but it seemed to strengthen Hairy's resolve.

"You're bluffing," he challenged, his head coming up defiantly. "We've got all the captains on board. Even if you could do it, you wouldn't just—"

"Good-bye, Hairy," Tambu said, lowering his hand to the console's keyboard.

For a split second, Hairy's face filled the screen, his eyes wide with terror. Then, for the second time that day, the screen went blank.

Immediately, Tambu rekeyed the display, and the view of the fleet reappeared—the fleet minus the Scorpion. There was no trace left of the meeting ship.

The console's board lit up like a Christmas tree. The blinking red lights chased each other up and down the board as Tambu sat and stared. Idly he noted in his mind which ships took the longest to call in.

Finally, his mind focused and he lunged forward, gripping the mike with one hand as his other played rapidly over the console's keyboard.

"This is Tambu," he announced. "All ships, cancel

your calls and stand by for a fleetwide announcement."

He waited as the call lights winked out.

"There has been an explosion of unknown origin on board the *Scorpion*," he announced. "We can only assume there are no survivors."

He paused for a moment to allow the message to sink in.

"First officers are to assume command of their vessels immediately," he ordered. "You are to take the rest of the day for whatever services you wish to perform for the lost personnel. Starting at 0800 hours tomorrow, I will contact each of you individually to assist in reorganizing your crews as well as to issue specific orders and assignments. Those ships closest to the *Scorpion* have one hour to conduct a damage inspection of their ships. After that, they are to call me with a status report. Acknowledge receipt of message by responding with an amber call."

He watched as the board lit up again. This time the lights were all amber—all but one. The *Scorpion* would never call in again.

"Tambu out."

The fleet secure, Tambu slumped back in his chair as the enormity of his deed washed over him.

Gone! All of them. Ramona, Egor, A.C., Jelly . . . all of them wiped out when he pressed a single button on his console.

In his shock-dulled mind, he realized he had lost his personal battle. When pressured, it was Tambu who controlled his actions, and Tambu had ended his last hope of retirement. He couldn't leave the fleet now. With the captains gone, there would be no one to pass control to. He would have to stay on, working with the new captains, reorganizing . . .

He had lost. He was Tambu.

The horror of that realization rose up and sucked him down . . . Tambu wept.

INTERVIEW XII

"I transferred ships shortly after that. I found my old quarters held too many memories for comfort. That pretty much brings us to the present. For the last two years, I have been training the new captains. The Council is now established and functioning, allowing me leisure time, which in turn enabled me to grant you this interview."

"And the fleet never found out the actual cause of the explosion on the *Scorpion*?" Erickson asked.

"Of course they found out. I told each of the new captains during their initial briefing. I felt it was a necessary lesson as to the possible repercussions of a poor captain-crew relationship."

"Didn't anyone question what you had done?" the reporter pressed. "I mean, surely someone objected to your handling of the situation."

"Remember our discussion of famous people, Mr. Erickson," Tambu instructed. "None of the new captains had ever dealt directly with me before. They had been suddenly thrust into a new position of responsibility, and were casting about for direction and approval. Preconditioned to view me with awe and fear, they readily accepted me as their authority figure, the only one between them and chaos. No one questioned my actions, but they eagerly learned the lesson of the disaster."

"Of course, you've done nothing to encourage that awe and fear," Erickson said.

"Quite the opposite," Tambu admitted easily. "I've done everything I could to build the image. Most of my work for the last two years has been establishing and maintaining the gap between myself and the fleet."

"But why?" the reporter asked. "It seems you're not only accepting your isolation, you're creating it."

"Well put, Mr. Erickson. As to why I'm doing this, remember the *Scorpion* episode. I lost a ship, a good crew, and all my captains because I had allowed my judgment to be clouded by personal friendship. I have found I function much more efficiently in isolation. As I started this latest phase without friends or confidants, it has been relatively easy to avoid forming any. I feel my judgments and appraisals have benefited from this detachment."

"Have you taken a new mistress?" Erickson said bluntly.

"No," Tambu replied after a moment's pause. "I make no pretensions of loyalty to Ramona's memory. I have no doubts that eventually I will need someone again, but it's still too soon."

"It occurred to me earlier in the interview, but now that I've heard your whole story, I feel I must make the observation out loud: You pay a terrible price for your position, Tambu."

"Don't pity me, Mr. Erickson." Tambu's voice was cold. "I do what I do willingly—just as you accept travel, cheap rooms, and restaurant food as a necessary part of your chosen occupation. Once, when I thought of stepping down, I felt regret and remorse. I mentioned at the end of that episode, however, that battle has been won—or lost, depending on your point of view. I am Tambu now, and I do what is necessary to be Tambu. I was born in the early days of the fleet's formation, and the fleet is my life now."

"Then you have no plans for retirement now that the Council is ready to assume command?" Erickson asked.

"Retire to what?" Tambu countered. "My family is dead. My friends are dead. There's nothing for me outside of the fleet."

"That's pretty definite," the reporter acknowledged. "What about the future? What do you see ahead for you and the fleet? A continuance of the status quo?"

"Nothing is forever, Mr. Erickson. The only certain thing in the universe is change. The specifics are anybody's guess. The Defense Alliance is growing larger every year. They may eventually feel they are strong enough to attempt a direct confrontation. I think it would be stupid of them to try it, but they've come a long way doing things I thought were stupid. Then again, they may simply crowd us out of the starlanes."

"You seem unconcerned about either possibility."

Tambu laughed. "If you want my real prediction of the future, I fully expect to slip on a bar of soap and crack my head open in the shower. I've led far too exciting a life to be able to expect anything but an anticlimactic death. But whatever happens in the future, I am the fleet. If I die, the fleet dies with me, and vice versa. I'll leave it to the Fates to work out the details."

"A fitting epitaph," Erickson smiled. "Well, while I could sit here for days talking with you, I've got to admit I have more than enough material for my article."

"Very well, Mr. Erickson. It has been a rare pleasure talking with you these last few hours. Can you remember the way back to the docking bay where your ship is, or shall I call for a guide?"

"I can remember the way. Just give me a moment to gather my things."

"If you don't mind, Mr. Erickson, may I ask you a question before you go?"

"Certainly," the reporter blinked. "What would you like to know?"

"Solely to satisfy my own curiosity, I'd like to know what you intend to say in your article."

A shiver of apprehension ran down Erickson's spine. The alienness of his surroundings came back to him with a rush, as did the distance he had to cover to reach his ship and safety. Taking a deep breath, he turned and faced the blank viewscreen directly.

"I'm going to try to tell your story as I see it," he said carefully. "It's the story of a forceful man with a dream, a dream that went awry and carried him with it."

He paused for a moment, but there was no rebuttal from the screen.

"The man had an incredible sense of loyalty and obligation," he continued haltingly, " a sense of loyalty so strong, it blinded him to everything else in the universe and in his mind. First he was loyal to his friends, then to the planets, and finally to the fleet . . . the business he had built. At each step, his sense of obligation was so strong, so single-minded, that it was beyond the comprehension of everyone who came in contact with him. There were people all along the way who might have swayed him from his course, but they couldn't understand what was happening, and instead of helping, actually speeded him on his way with their actions. It's the story of a man who gave so much of himself that now there's nothing human left—just the image he built with the aid of those who supported or opposed him. That's the story I intend to write, sir . . . assuming, of course, I'm allowed to leave the ship with my notes, mind, and body intact."

"That's an interesting story," Tambu said after a moment's silence. "I'll look forward to seeing it in its final form. I don't agree with all your observations, but, even if I took exception to the entire story, you would be allowed to leave. I granted you an interview and a newsman's immunity, Mr. Erickson. There were no conditions about whether or not I would like what you wrote. If I had wanted my own opinions printed, I would have simply written the article myself and released it to the news services."

"But you still controlled what you did and didn't tell me," Erickson pointed out. "I remember that earlier in our conversation, you stated that anyone being interviewed would slant the facts to create a certain impression. Would you tell me now, off the record, how much of what you've said was exaggerated or downplayed to further your own image?"

"You'll never know that for certain, Mr. Erickson. But if you're willing to believe me at all, accept that I have not knowingly slanted anything. You see, I feel that actions and reactions have been colorful enough without exaggeration. Then, too, there's the fact that I sincerely believe your article will not affect me or the fleet in any way—positive or negative. Our supporters and decriers will accept or reject different portions of your accounts depending on their preformed conception of our motives and activities. Perhaps if I truly believed your article would change people's minds, I might have become concerned enough to lie to you; but as it stands, the truth can be no more damaging to the fleet than any fabrication."

"But if my article really means so little to you, why did you bother giving me the interview at all?"

"I told you at the beginning of our conversation. Curiosity. As one who has been branded as the archvillain of contemporary times, I was curious to meet and have a prolonged conversation with someone who believes in heroes and villains. That same curiosity prompts me to ask you one more question. During our talk, you have shown both distaste and sympathy for me. I ask you now, in your opinion, am I a villain?"

Erickson frowned.

"I don't know," he admitted finally. "While I still believe in evil, I'm no longer sure of its definition. Is evil inherent in the deed, or in the intent? If it's in the deed, then you're a villain. Too many bodies can be laid at your doorstep to be ignored. Of course, if that's our sole unit of measure, then every honored general from mankind's history must be burning in hell right now."

"You are quite correct," Tambu acknowledged. "I personally tend to judge myself on a basis of intent. By that measure, I feel no guilt over my career. I wonder how many people could make the same claim? Yourself, Mr. Erickson. During our interview, I've observed you waging war with yourself—the man versus the professional. You've been constantly struggling to impose 'what you should say' over 'what you would like to say.' In that, your dilemma is not unlike my own Eisner-Tambu difficulties."

"You're quite observant," Erickson acknowledged, "but I'd like to think I'm not the only one with that problem. I'm sure a lot of reporters suffer the same dilemma."

"A lot of *people* suffer the same dilemma," Tambu corrected. "I was not attempting to criticize you. I was trying to point out that many people feel the need to sacrifice their normal inclinations to conform to their chosen professions. I would hazard a prophecy that if you continue with your career as a reporter, the day will come when your personal questions or statements will not even enter your mind during an interview. You will conduct yourself consciously and subconsciously as a journalist—and on that day you will have become a journalist just as I have become Tambu."

"You may be right." Erickson shrugged. "However,

the standards and ethics of my profession were set long before I entered the field; and if I adhere to them, there is little or no chance I will gain your infamy. Remember, sir, you set your own standards and must therefore bear the full weight of their consequences."

"I can't deny that," Tambu admitted, "either the setting of standards or the responsibility for them. However, we were speaking of intent and guilt. Though branded a villain, throughout my career, I have acted with what in my mind were the purest of intentions. All too frequently the results went awry, but each decision made was, in my judgment, made in favor of the greatest good for others, not for myself—and was therefore in keeping with my personal ethics. That is the salve I have to use against any doubts or feelings of guilt. Do you have that same salve, Mr. Erickson? Can you say that in your career as a reporter you've never betrayed a confidence, cheated a friend, or broken a promise for the sake of a story? That you've never gone against your own principles to further your career? That you've never allowed your self-interest to overshadow your ethics?"

The reporter dropped his eyes and frowned thoughtfully, but did not answer.

Tambu concluded, "Then I ask you, Mr. Erickson, who is the bigger villain? You or I?"

MURDER, MAYHEM, SKULDUGGERY... AND A CAST OF CHARACTERS YOU'LL NEVER FORGET!

THIEVES' WORLD™

EDITED BY
ROBERT LYNN ASPRIN and LYNN ABBEY

FANTASTICAL ADVENTURES

One Thumb, the crooked bartender at the Vulgar Unicorn...*Enas Yorl,* magician and shape changer ...*Jubal,* ex-gladiator and crime lord...*Lythande the Star-browed,* master swordsman and would-be wizard...these are just a few of the players you will meet in a mystical place called Sanctuary. This is *Thieves' World.* Enter with care.

__80583-3	THIEVES' WORLD	$2.95
__79580-3	TALES FROM THE VULGAR UNICORN	$2.95
__76031-7	SHADOWS OF SANCTUARY	$2.95
__78712-6	STORM SEASON	$2.95
__22550-0	THE FACE OF CHAOS	$2.95
__80594-9	WINGS OF OMEN	$2.95

Prices may be slightly higher in Canada.

Available at your local bookstore or return this form to:

 ACE SCIENCE FICTION
Book Mailing Service
P.O. Box 690, Rockville Centre, NY 11571

Please send me the titles checked above. I enclose _____. Include 75¢ for postage and handling if one book is ordered; 25¢ per book for two or more not to exceed $1.75. California, Illinois, New York and Tennessee residents please add sales tax.

NAME_____

ADDRESS_____

CITY_____STATE/ZIP_____

(allow six weeks for delivery)

SF 2

EXCITING SCIENCE FICTION BESTSELLERS!

____ **STRANGER IN A STRANGE LAND**
Robert A. Heinlein   08094-3 — $3.95

____ **THE MOON IS A HARSH MISTRESS**
Robert A. Heinlein   08100-1 — $3.50

____ **GOD EMPEROR OF DUNE**
Frank Herbert   08003-X — $3.95

____ **CHILDREN OF DUNE**
Frank Herbert   07499-4 — $3.95

____ **DUNE**
Frank Herbert   08002-1 — $3.95

____ **DUNE MESSIAH**
Frank Herbert   07498-6 — $3.95

____ **THE BOOK OF MERLYN**
T. H. White   07282-7 — $2.95

____ **THE ONCE AND FUTURE KING**
T. H. White   08196-6 — $4.50

____ **WIZARD**
John Varley   08166-4 — $3.50

____ **TITAN**
John Varley   07320-3 — $2.95

Prices may be slightly higher in Canada.

Available at your local bookstore or return this form to:

Ⓑ BERKLEY
Book Mailing Service
P.O. Box 690, Rockville Centre, NY 11571

Please send me the titles checked above. I enclose _____ Include 75¢ for postage and handling if one book is ordered; 25¢ per book for two or more not to exceed $1.75. California, Illinois, New York and Tennessee residents please add sales tax.

NAME _____

ADDRESS _____

CITY _____ STATE/ZIP_____

(allow six weeks for delivery)

23J

Magikal mirth'n mayhem from the creator of Thieves' World™

Make no mythstake, this is the wildest, wackiest, most frolicking fantasy series around. With the mythfit Skeeve and his magical mythadventures, Aahz the pervert demon, Gleep the baby dragon, and a crazy cast of mythstifying characters, Robert Asprin's "Myth" series is a guaranteed good time. Join the world of deveels, dragons and magik—and join the wacky adventures of fantasy's most fun-loving mythfits.

_02360-6 Another Fine Myth $2.95
_55519-5 Myth Conceptions $2.95
_55525-X Myth Directions $2.95
_33850-X Hit or Myth $2.95
          Available in
          September 1985

Prices may be slightly higher in Canada.

Available at your local bookstore or return this form to:

ACE
Book Mailing Service
P.O. Box 690, Rockville Centre, NY 11571

Please send me the titles checked above. I enclose _____. Include 75¢ for postage and handling if one book is ordered; 25¢ per book for two or more not to exceed $1.75. California, Illinois, New York and Tennessee residents please add sales tax.

NAME_____

ADDRESS_____

CITY_____STATE/ZIP_____

(Allow six weeks for delivery.)   400/A

BESTSELLING
Science Fiction
and
Fantasy

☐ 47810-7	**THE LEFT HAND OF DARKNESS,** Ursula K. Le Guin	$2.95
☐ 16021-2	**DORSAI!,** Gordon R. Dickson	$2.95
☐ 80583-3	**THIEVES' WORLD,™** Robert Lynn Asprin, editor	$2.95
☐ 11456-3	**CONAN #1,** Robert E. Howard, L. Sprague de Camp, Lin Carter	$2.75
☐ 49142-1	**LORD DARCY INVESTIGATES,** Randall Garrett	$2.75
☐ 21889-X	**EXPANDED UNIVERSE,** Robert A. Heinlein	$3.95
☐ 87330-8	**THE WARLOCK UNLOCKED,** Christopher Stasheff	$2.95
☐ 05490-0	**BERSERKER,** Fred Saberhagen	$2.95
☐ 10264-6	**CHANGELING,** Roger Zelazny	$2.95
☐ 51553-3	**THE MAGIC GOES AWAY,** Larry Niven	$2.95

Prices may be slightly higher in Canada.

Available at your local bookstore or return this form to:

ACE SCIENCE FICTION
Book Mailing Service
P.O. Box 690, Rockville Centre, NY 11571

Please send me the titles checked above. I enclose _____. Include 75¢ for postage and handling if one book is ordered; 25¢ per book for two or more not to exceed $1.75. California, Illinois, New York and Tennessee residents please add sales tax.

NAME_____

ADDRESS_____

CITY_____STATE/ZIP_____

(allow six weeks for delivery)   **SF 9**